To the real RJ,
a true inspiration.
(She told me to write that)

Prologue

She moved silently, closing in on her prey, her feet automatically seeking out soft patches of ground on which to tread. The gently dimming light of the evening aided in concealing her. Gorse, tufts of grass, the uneven terrain, and the fact that she was cloaked fully in black, ensured she could remain hidden. The midge—the bane of the Scottish countryside—her only disadvantage as she strove to remain still under their incessant onslaught.

She'd done this many times, but never before had her prey hunted her in turn. Not that she knew of, at least.

The man she was watching lifted the scope of his rifle and panned slowly across the face of a hill in the distance—where she had been positioned only an hour ago. If he had arrived sooner, perhaps their fates would now be reversed. Unluckily for him, she was much more accomplished at the hunt than he was.

When she had a job to do such as this, it consumed her. She had taken down too many to remember but had learned from each and every one of them, honing her skills over the years. She was nothing short of a killing machine; he had no chance of getting out of this alive—she didn't doubt her abilities for a second.

The others had underestimated her, as had the hunter in front of her. Thinking her an easy target would be his downfall.

Seeing nothing through his scope, he began his descent, concentrating on his footfalls lest he slip or turn his ankle on a rock. He stopped every few meters and held the scope to his eye, searching for her, unaware that she had him clearly in her own sights.

Unable to follow him directly down the hill without giving away her position, she circled round, attempting to find the best point of attack, aware that she might only have one shot. She had to get close. It was her modus operandi. Though the strategy wasn't without its risks, it had paid off countless times before. If she was too far away, there was no guarantee she would take him down and he might escape; too close and he might take her. It was always the second risk she favored.

She edged her way nearer, parallel to her prey, ensuring she was neither above nor below his position. She was almost there, almost ready, almost at an optimum distance when he stopped walking.

Perhaps sensing her presence, her hunter stood still, turning back the way he had come. Suddenly, he stiffened and, although upwind, she could almost smell his fear. He knew she was there, knew what was about to happen. He turned around and looked directly at her, fumbling frantically for his gun before his head exploded in a shower of red.

Covering the corpse, she walked away with a deep sense of satisfaction thrumming through her entire body.

Jo McCready

Chapter 1

Governor Kowalski ran a hand through his thinning hair and pushed it back in place. He picked up the phone from his leather-covered desk and dialed the number on the card he held. A card he'd had little reason to use since it was given to him seven years previously, when he was first elected. The card had been hidden in plain sight in his rolodex, which he had never got around to digitizing—or rather had his secretary digitize it for him. He wasn't unusual in that aspect amongst his peers. 'Old School' he'd often heard them called by the younger set. He had no problems with the term, rather he embraced it. He had been elected due to his good old-fashioned family values, after all. Values he held dear. Values he was either about to compromise or protect with this call.

"Good morning, you've reached Kingfisher. How may I direct your call?" asked a woman with a sweet Southern drawl that reminded him of Dolly Parton in some ridiculous way.

"Is Benjamin Stone still in charge?" Kowalski asked. Was he doing the right thing?

"Yes, Governor. Please hold and I'll put you through."

Michael Kowalski moved the cell phone from his ear and stared at it. How in the hell had they known who was calling? He'd purchased the phone at the airport in Dulles the previous night before he'd returned home and had paid with cash so there would be nothing to link him to the purchase.

He returned it to his ear and waited.

"Governor, how can I be of assistance to you?" came the smooth and dulcet tones of Benjamin Stone. They'd never met in person, but the governor recognized his voice from the few times in the past when he'd had to make contact. It was Benjamin Stone who had initially reached out all those years ago to inform him of the organization and what it could do if needed. At first, the newly appointed governor had thought someone was playing an elaborate prank on him, but he soon found out the scope of the organization when Kingfisher helped to retrieve one of his constituents from a hostage situation in Somalia—a desperate situation in which the government had refused to help. The power and resources of the organization had both impressed and intimidated the governor, and he was glad he'd had no further call to use their services . . . until today.

"I'll cut to the chase, Mr. Stone. My brother-in law James Sullivan. You'll have seen the news, no doubt."

"I do recall something concerning Mr. Sullivan's sudden demise while vacationing in Scotland a few months ago. Is that correct?"

"Indeed, Mr. Stone. Indeed, it is."

"A fall, that's what was reported, was it not?"

There had been numerous headlines and banners running across the bottom of the news channels when the incident had occurred. *Tech billionaire dies tragically in cliff fall while on vacation in Scotland.* It didn't seem too far out of the realm of possibilities. Being rich didn't shield anyone from death—death simply found another mechanism to seize his rich clientele. Balloon accidents, helicopter- and- plane crashes, drug overdoses, and, in the case of one of Benjamin's recent client's, a death faked in order for a world-renowned rock star to reclaim his life.

"That's what we were told, yes," replied the governor.

Silence descended upon the line as Benjamin waited for the governor to elaborate. He didn't have to wait long.

"Mr. Stone, I don't believe James died from accidental causes."

Benjamin had suspected as much the moment he had heard that Governor Kowalski was on the line. In fact, he had expected a phone call much sooner. Something about the news hadn't rung true when he'd heard it. He had an ear for those things, a cynical eye which he cast over all that he experienced. Nothing was ever as it seemed. Benjamin had been in the business long enough to know that what was portrayed to the outside world was rarely an accurate expression of the truth. It simply served a purpose. The truth was never a priority for most.

"Can I ask what gives you reason for your suspicions, Governor?"

"There was a mix up. Rather, we were told there was a mix up with the morgue and the funeral home. He was cremated before we got there. The coffin on the news, when he was repatriated, was empty. I carried his ashes back in a box in my briefcase. At the time, we were all in shock, and it didn't occur to anyone that there was anything untoward. I spoke to the procurator fiscal—their equivalent of a coroner. I read the report. I believed it all, even without any actual physical evidence in front of me. We had no reason to doubt the situation as it was described to us."

"And now?"

"Now, Mr. Stone, I have the benefit of hindsight. Plus, now that my sister has finally calmed down enough to function, she has begun to sort through the estate. Well, she has someone to do that for her. A few . . . anomalies have cropped up in my brother-in-law's financials."

Benjamin sat straighter in his chair. "Anomalies? How so?"

"Over the last three months, there have been weekly payments of five thousand dollars wired to an account in the Caymans. Janice knows nothing about these payments, and no one in his inner circle can attribute them to anything, be it business or personal transactions."

"It could, of course, be perfectly innocent and unrelated to his death."

"I don't think you believe that any more than I do, Mr. Stone." Michael Kowalski's tone was hard and devoid of emotion.

"Perhaps. What's your theory on this, Governor?"

Kowalski's right knee shook under his desk as he considered, yet again, what he was about to do. "I think he may have been paying someone off. I think someone was blackmailing him."

"You must realize that the sums are very insubstantial for someone of his wealth?"

"I can't explain that, but something is off about this whole thing. If his death was intentional, I want to find out why. It's imperative that we find out what really happened, for my sister's peace of mind, at least."

There was something the governor wasn't saying, Benjamin was sure of it. "Was there anything in your brother-in-law's life that might have led to anyone blackmailing him?"

"Not that we knew of, or can find. He'd recently set up a charity foundation for children from disadvantaged backgrounds. He grew up in the slums himself, as you well know. Clawed himself up with sheer tenacity and a genius that surprised everybody, not least himself. He was a standup guy. Didn't lie, didn't cheat. His businesses were all legit. I can't think of a single reason someone might blackmail him and certainly no reason for wanting him dead. People were envious of him, sure, and he did butt heads with other big tech companies and the government at times. Nothing that could conceivably lead to his death, though. Nothing I can see anyway."

"And yet you think his death was suspicious?"

The governor blew out a breath. "Something doesn't add up. First the cremation, and now the money."

"You mentioned that you read the procurator fiscal's report?"

"Yes."

"You realize if there was a cover up, a great deal of people would need to be involved over there, not least the fiscal himself?"

"Yes, and I can think of no reason why that would be, but, by implication, the answer lies in Scotland."

"I can see how circumstances could lead you to that conclusion," Benjamin replied. He'd already considered the possibility. It wasn't the only possibility, however. "Is it possible anyone from his past is involved? An incident that you don't know about, precipitating his death?"

The line went silent for a moment.

"I don't believe so, but it's certainly possible," Kowalski said. "I don't see how anyone from his distant past would have the means to do that. James climbed out of that life at a young age, met and married my sister while still at college. Not long after, he sold his first company for two-hundred-and-fifty million dollars. As for things I don't know about, I couldn't even begin to imagine what that might be. You have to understand, James was a very busy man. His entire day was planned, his every move diarized. If he wasn't with business associates or employees, he was with my sister . . . his wife. His work was his life, and that life started early. He didn't have a past, not one I knew about."

"I'm sorry, Governor, but I have to ask. Your sister . . . ?"

"Let's get one thing straight, right off the bat, Mr. Stone. I don't like what you're implying, and I urge you very strongly not to go down that route. I'm coming to you for help, not to get my family dragged through the mud."

"I apologize for the difficult question, Governor. We have to ensure we have all available information if we are to get you the answers you seek. Sometimes that simply means eliminating potential lines of enquiry at the outset. The more we know, the easier it is for us to do our job."

"I understand," said Governor Kowalski, his tone softer than before. "My sister loved her husband more than life itself, and I don't believe he'd ever have an affair. Their adoration always appeared to be mutual." He sighed inwardly at intrusion of having to give someone such personal information. It was humiliating.

Benjamin let the issue go for the moment. He had seen the wool pulled over people's eyes for years when it came to their nearest and dearest. The more a person was described as an open book, the more skeletons they had hidden in their closets. Often, those closest to them were the most gullible to their charms. He'd have a team do some diplomatic digging.

"Any health issues, physical or psychological?"

"None."

"That you know of," Benjamin prompted.

"That we know of," the governor agreed.

"I must ask you, why call us? Why not use your own influence to reopen the case or hire a private investigator?"

"I don't know what I'm dealing with yet, Mr. Stone. I require discretion and an assurance that you will find the truth. I can't trust any other parties to guarantee that. Also, if the procurator fiscal is involved, I don't know how high up this goes. A private investigator or my own investigations are likely to be unsuccessful. I appreciate that your organization has some resources and techniques that are not widely available. You're my best bet in getting to the truth. Whatever that is, I want to know. My family needs to know."

"I understand, Governor. We will get to the bottom of this, I can assure you. Of course, it is possible that his death is completely unrelated to the money. However, I agree that you are right to be concerned. I'll have a team briefed immediately."

"I appreciate your help with this, Mr. Stone. This entire thing has been a living nightmare. I can count on your discretion, of course. I'm sure I don't need to tell you that this is . . . delicate?"

"As always," Benjamin reassured him. "Governor, I have read the news reports, but if you could tell me yourself, why was your brother-in-law in Scotland?"

"He was hunting."

Chapter 2

Benjamin got up from his desk and walked to his window. He stood staring, both through the glass and through the scene beyond, seeing nothing of the view outside the window. He bunched his hands into fists on his hips as he stood rooted to the spot. He had a feeling that the governor was hiding something from him. Rubbing his chin, he considered what that could mean for any potential investigation. He understood why Governor Kowalski had come to Kingfisher. They were virtually untraceable, after all. Involving a government body would only have caused problems and wouldn't get him the answers he needed. Far better to approach an organization with a wider and longer reach. Some people might think of them as mercenaries, but they had a robust ethical committee when it came to deciding which assignments to accept. This one was straightforward enough for Benjamin to accept on behalf of Kingfisher without the need to go through that process.

Luckily for Benjamin and the rest of the Kingfisher team stationed all over the world, there was plenty of corruption, political intrigue, high-level smuggling and industrial espionage to keep them more than busy—and unashamedly financially secure. Every now and then, an assignment would come along that drifted from the norm enough to be interesting. It was these cases that had kept Benjamin Stone in the game after all these years. Looking into James Sullivan's death would be nothing if not interesting.

Gathering his thoughts, he returned to his desk, pressing the intercom buzzer for his assistant Martha as he sat down.

Martha appeared at his door moments later, and he invited her to sit. Her manicured silver-gray bob didn't move a millimeter as she gracefully folded into the seat in front of him, her notebook and pen at the ready in her lap

"It seems we have a transatlantic situation that requires our attention." He proceeded to explain the situation, just as the governor had detailed over the phone.

"Have Macy put together a team. Tracing the financial transactions is the first priority. We need access to the procurator fiscal's report and the police report. Someone needs to interview the widow. We need complete access to everything we can find out about James Sullivan, past and present, including his most recent vacation details. Look into his family members, including Governor Kowalski. Something doesn't sit quite right there."

"Do you have a preference for the agent on the ground over there?" Martha asked.

"We have a few options. But first, get me RJ's most recent psych evaluation. Don't look at me like that, Martha," he said as she looked up from her notes and stared at him. Before RJ came along, Martha was the only person in the organization who dared question Benjamin's authority.

Martha pursed her lips and said nothing, her concern showing in her raised eyebrows and her unwavering stare.

"I won't send her unless both she and the psychologist give the okay."

Martha continued her disarming scrutiny. She was tougher than many of the agents he sent out in the field but not quite a match for the man in charge, even if she liked to believe she was.

The heavy silence burned through Benjamin's skull, and he felt a migraine forming. It wasn't that Martha intimidated him; it was the thought of sending RJ on this particular assignment. He'd stopped assassination attempts, recovered priceless artifacts, been shot at, risked his life too many times to remember, all without breaking a sweat—but the thought of putting his only family in this position was almost enough to break his cool.

"Yes, I know RJ will say its fine for her to be over there, and yes, I know how dangerous psychological distractions can be in the field, but, damn it, do you really think I would send my own niece over there if I thought I was putting her in real danger?"

Martha's left eyebrow lifted almost imperceptibly.

"Yes, yes, I know the irony of me saying that as all our missions are dangerous in one way or another. I'm not making any decisions until I get more data, but it makes the most sense for RJ to be the agent we send."

Martha's nostrils flared slightly as she blew a deep breath out of her nose and stood up to leave. "I'll get Macy to work right away, and get the psych report to you in a few minutes."

"Thank you." At the moment, Benjamin despised her for being his moral compass. His head was already almost bursting at the thought of sending RJ over to Scotland, but if he was to think like the director that he was, there was little choice in the matter. Her accent and knowledge—the fact that she'd lived there most of her life—made her the most logical choice to go in undercover. Her issues with returning to the country of her birth, however, might very well outweigh that hefty advantage.

His computer pinged, signaling that he'd received an email. Martha, as efficient as always, had sent through the psych evaluation within minutes of leaving his office. He opened it and read through the summary, looking for anything he should be worried about.

Coping well after first mission and appears to have settled into role. No kills to date. Unable to ascertain at this moment the effect this would have on agent's state of mind. Has reconciled with the idea that parents worked for the organization in the past. I'm of the belief, as is the agent in question, that this new role as well as the information about her parents and surviving family has aided in her grieving process. I have no hesitation in recommending this agent for further duties in the field or otherwise.

Benjamin scanned through the rest of the report, finding nothing more of any interest. It was bordering on unethical—him reading the psych evaluation of a family member. There was certainly a conflict of interest, no one could argue against that. It was a necessary invasion, though, and one RJ knew about and had consented to. Benjamin had access to all employee data should he need it. But with RJ, he had responsibilities that extended far beyond his role as director. He was her uncle; her only family member—the only person left to look out for her and keep her safe. He would do that any way possible with all information available to him.

RJ shouldn't have been able to mislead the psychologist. The report was written after hours of observations, mission notes, and discussions with colleagues—not solely individual therapy sessions. He wouldn't be sure, though, until he looked in RJ's eyes and saw it for himself.

#

RJ had just finished a grueling physical evaluation and was taking a much-anticipated steam shower when she heard her phone beep. She put her hand out through the curtain, searching blindly for her cell. Glancing at the screen, she saw it was a text from her uncle asking her to meet him in his office in thirty minutes, and she relaxed in the knowledge that she had time to ease her tired muscles and get herself together. She rubbed at the indentations on her face from the mask that had been used to measure the oxygen circulating through her body. Her oxygen rates were much higher than when she'd first joined the organization, her heart rate quicker to return to normal and her strength vastly increased, but God, she hated those tests. They always pushed her to her limits, albeit those limits were now increased, but she always ended up feeling like she was going to pass out from the exertion. She'd rather go ten rounds with Ivan, her hand-to-hand combat trainer who regularly whooped her ass and left her covered in bruises, than endure another bloody physical evaluation again. Even though she did get a sense of satisfaction and achievement when she saw her results afterwards, it sure as hell wasn't worth it.

She lathered her hair, the soft scent of her expensive shampoo invading her senses and lulling her tight muscles into relaxation. It was one of the only luxuries she allowed herself. Good food and quality personal care items. She deserved both after the mental and physical torture they put her through at headquarters—today being a prime example.

Reluctantly, she rinsed the soapy suds from her hair and body, then turned the shower off. She dried herself with the large, fluffy white towel provided, dressed quickly and dried her straight hair with the powerful hairdryer on the dresser in the bathroom. There was no way she could walk about the floors above without being anything less than well put together. The agents there might walk around with split lips, black eyes, and goodness knows what else, but God forbid they have even a hair out of place. They were expected to hold themselves to professional standards at all times. RJ still hadn't decided whether this conventional attitude in the organization was a good thing or not.

"Agents are expected to give a hundred percent at all times in all ways," her uncle had once explained to her. "Our employees are the best of the best. We don't expect perfection, but we expect you to strive damn well near to it."

RJ understood—she did—but keeping up those standards day after day was exhausting. She knew it was good practice for being out in the field, though, and she really did try her best. That's where her competitive nature came in handy. She hadn't seen anyone else's professionalism slip, so she wasn't about to let hers do so.

As she made her way up to her uncle's office, her spine tingled in anticipation. She might be about to receive a new assignment, only her second to date. The first one had been a bit of a washout. She hoped she could finally get something to stick her teeth into, something to put her newly acquired skills to the test. Her previous life as a geology professor was long gone, but it felt as though she was waiting in the wings for the new one to start. This meeting would hopefully change that. If Ben had wanted to see her for personal reasons, he would have waited to talk to her at home that evening. They were both working hard to keep that separation clear—their relationship at the organization was strictly professional; at home they were family.

"Afternoon, RJ," Martha, the gatekeeper to her uncle's inner sanctum, greeted her. "Go straight through, he's expecting you."

RJ smiled her thanks but hesitated at the older lady's desk. Everyone knew she was the real force behind the organization. She shared a connection with her uncle's assistant in that they were the only two people in the organization who could, and regularly did, question his authority.

"How are you, Martha?" RJ asked her.

Martha's expression didn't change, but RJ noticed a subtle shift in her eye movements. Perhaps she was surprised that an agent cared enough to ask about her. Although, RJ could imagine the handsome ones trying and failing to use their charms to get on Martha's good side. It simply wouldn't happen. RJ just knew Martha would never give them an inch.

"I'm very fine, thank you, RJ. And, how are you? How's the training going?" Martha never gave much away about herself, but it didn't stop RJ from trying to find a chink in her armor.

"Urgh!" RJ groaned, rolling her eyes. "I had my fitness test this morning. This job certainly has its ups and downs, but between you and me, I much prefer being out on assignment."

"You all do, dear," Martha assured her with a steely smile.

RJ nodded. She'd spent a lot of time at HQ during her training period and had seen how stir-crazy the agents could get when they were here, waiting for the next job and updating their skills. The young ones, like her, were especially keen to get out into the field, and though the more experienced agents were more aware of the dangers that awaited them with each new assignment, there was still a restlessness evident in them whenever they were stuck at HQ between assignments.

"I'm hoping that's what I'm here for now, a new assignment. Do you know anything?"

"You'll have to talk to Benjamin about that."

"But you do know, right?"

Martha simply smiled. Try as she might, RJ could never get anything out of her. People at Kingfisher were just too damn good at their jobs. She'd just have to find out from the man in charge. RJ shook her head and gave Martha one last smile as she headed to Benjamin's office.

She pushed open the door to see her uncle at his desk, fingers steepled and his Newton's cradle rocking on his desk—a sure sign that he had been deep in thought on a weighty issue.

"Hey," she greeted him, tilting her chin up in greeting.

He looked her straight in the eye, unsmiling. "Hey."

It was not a reassuring sight. RJ's guard immediately went up.

"Uh-oh, what've I done now?" she joked in an attempt to hide her trepidation.

"I don't know, why don't you tell me?"

"Um . . ."

"Don't look so worried, RJ, that's not why I've called you here." He waved a hand in dismissal. "I am intrigued about what you may have done to make you look so guilty, but that'll have to wait."

"So, why did you want to see me? And I haven't done anything, Uncle Ben. It's just the effect of being called to the 'headmaster's office'. I can assure you I've been handing all my homework in and have been really good in class. Ask any of my teachers." She tried to look contrite but could see he wasn't buying it.

"Believe me, I'd know if you haven't. I'm well aware how well you have been doing. That's part of the reason you're here. I wanted to talk to you about a new assignment." He took a breath that anyone else would have missed, but RJ was so familiar with him, she couldn't fail to notice.

"I figured as much. You don't look very happy about it, though." She leaned forward in her chair, her back suddenly straighter and her ears on high alert. "So, what's the deal with the assignment? What's got you so worried?"

"The assignment lends itself particularly well to your unique set of skills. I have every confidence in your abilities . . ."

RJ waited but he didn't continue. His face was inscrutable. He didn't need to fill in the gaps. If there was nothing for her to worry about regarding the actual assignment, there could only be a handful of other issues that might make him so ill at ease.

"It's not the assignment, is it? It's the location." The realization hit RJ with a surprisingly dull ache.

"Well . . ." he began.

Chapter 3

RJ drove her rental car towards the Sullivans' summer house in New Hampshire, passing houses that grew progressively larger with each mile she traveled. The trees were in full splendor as they basked in their present status, the threat of autumn so out of reach that they almost seemed to dance with emerald joy.

She had been surprised at her uncle's request that she go on assignment in Scotland, but even more surprised at her own reaction. A trip that would have filled her with dread and trepidation merely a year ago was now viewed through eyes that saw it simply as a job, a task she was required to complete. She hadn't been able to cope with the idea of staying in Scotland after her parents' tragic death at the hands of a hit-and-run driver and had practically jumped at the chance to continue her academic career overseas. Up until now, she hadn't been able to face going back, had barely even given it any thought. Of course, the idea that she wouldn't have to see or interact with anyone she knew and would be a world away from her old hometown made it easier. The fact that she would be returning to an area where she had vacationed with her family as a young girl was unexpectedly comforting. It felt fitting that she would return there to perform a role both her parents had performed in the past—although, she hadn't known that until recently. She was actually excited at the prospect.

Ben, bless him, had looked like the weight of a mountain had been lifted from his shoulders at her reaction. He was worried about her, of course, she knew that, but for the first time in a long time, RJ felt grounded and capable of almost anything. She would feel eternally grateful that he had unwittingly forced her into an interview for Kingfisher and brought her into the fold that had once encompassed her parents. She'd felt like killing him when she'd found out that the perilous situation she'd been thrown into was nothing but a setup for her to join the organization, and that feeling hadn't subsided even when she'd discovered he was her dad's brother. Luckily for both of them, that anger had quickly given way to a bond that could never be broken, and an appreciation for a much more challenging and exciting life than her previous one in the world of geological academia. The idea that she was following in her parents' footsteps in what was effectively the family business of international espionage was just the icing on the cake.

The road gave way to an older surface laid with red bricks, and RJ reduced her speed. It wasn't clear if the road was historically important or if the local rich landowners had elected to have it built as a sign of prestige. Whatever the case, the necessary slower pace the bricks demanded helped as she looked for the number that had been given to her when the plane had landed a few hours previously.

Even at her reduced speed, she almost missed the driveway as she turned a corner under a mammoth weeping willow. She'd been too busy negotiating over the bricks that had been displaced by the tree's imposing root system to notice the break in the wall, hidden under the shadow of the tree. Skidding to a halt, she checked her rear-view mirror and backed up a few feet so she could enter the drive. The driveway wasn't designed to attract attention—you'd really need to know it was there or specifically be looking for it. The entrance consisted of a small break in what seemed like an impossibly long wall. A high, iron fence topped smooth, red brick walls—which looked to be from the same brickworks as the road—masking the high hedges within. It was more like a hidden lair or the back entrance to a sprawling property than the gaudy display of wealth RJ had expected. There was no indication as to who lived there—no name plates, no decoration on the fence or atop the gates, which were a simple extension of the fence—just a nondescript number stuck on the right-hand side of the flat, red wall that faced the road.

RJ pulled in and looked at the gates, which remained closed and unwelcoming. She glanced around until she spotted an unobtrusive intercom inlaid in the wall. It had been completely hidden until she was right alongside it, and even then, its existence wasn't obvious. When she pressed the call button, it was answered almost immediately. She had no doubt her every move was being watched through a camera hidden somewhere nearby.

"Yes?" a male voice answered. RJ assumed it was only one of a number of security personnel on the premises.

"RJ Rox for Ms. Janice Sullivan."

The imposing black gates slowly swung open, inviting RJ into the grounds. Hedges graced either side of the drive as she drove around a bend on the same brick paving until the material under her tires changed into crushed white shell. The drive curved around manicured grounds, showing off what must have been very expensive artwork at every bend. An impossibly tall-legged, blue elephant disappeared into the foliage behind her as she drove on, an enormous mosaic lion roared at her as she passed, and a shining metal giraffe sheltered her baby from the world. The artwork should have prepared RJ for what to expect when she saw the house, but when she turned the final corner to see the house displayed in front of her, she was flabbergasted. She pulled up alongside a fountain of clamoring bronze howler monkeys juxtaposed beside the red-brick façade of the most enormous house she had ever seen. Three stories stretched high into the air; the walls made up of as much glass as they were of brick.

Janice was waiting at the bottom of a sandstone staircase that led into the house.

"I don't care what you do with it, I told you I don't want it in my house," she hissed into her cell phone before abruptly terminating the call. Her face, once pretty, was red and blotchy, her eyes puffy and free of makeup. The only signs of extravagance RJ noted were the diamond studs in her ears and the rings on her wedding finger, which held an unexpectedly small and tasteful blue stone.

She stowed the cell in her pocket and looked at RJ with empty eyes. "James commissioned another piece for the garden before he died," she explained in lieu of greeting. “I can’t stand the thought of welcoming it with open arms.” She turned and started up the stairs, evidently expecting RJ to follow.

RJ complied, allowing herself to be led through the house.

“We’ll go through to the jetty. It’s so pretty at this time of year,” Janice said as she walked ahead, her voice monotone and almost robotic.

RJ took in the décor. If James Sullivan had decorated the sprawling grounds, then Janice had clearly been allowed free rein on the interior. The solid wood floors led to rooms filled with sumptuous sofas, antique furniture, and ornate chandeliers. One room held a grand piano, chaise lounge, and little else. Everything was understated yet obviously expensive—nothing like the attention-grabbing sculptures she had encountered on the drive.

Janice led her to the back of the house, down a path through what looked like an English country garden, and onto a wooden walkway over the water. The walkway opened out into an undercover lounge and dining area that overlooked a mirror-flat lake.

“Please sit.” Janice indicated a pair of rattan armchairs set in the shade without meeting RJ’s eyes.

"Ms. Sullivan, I am so very sorry for your loss. My name is RJ—"

"Yes, yes, I know. RJ Rox. I'm not entirely sure why Michael felt the need to hire a private investigator, but I'll answer any questions you might have as best as I can."

Benjamin had informed her that the widow believed she was a private investigator, and RJ was happy to play along.

"Lemonade?" Janice asked, her chest heaving as she sighed. Without waiting for a reply, Janice filled the lone glass on the table with lemonade and set it in front of RJ. Janice looked at her hands in her lap and picked at an already sore and bleeding bit of skin beside a chipped, French-manicured nail. Silent tears streaked her cheeks as she struggled to wrestle control. When she finally looked up, RJ saw eyes hidden in red, puffy wells—eyes that likely hadn't been dry in weeks.

"I still can't believe he's not coming back," she mumbled.

RJ waited. It was all she could do. She could offer no comfort to the woman in front of her, except to find out the truth.

Janice wiped her eyes on the sleeve of the light cashmere cardigan draped across her Pilates-sculpted, sun-browned shoulders, then took it off and used it to mop up the mucous that had built up under her nose. She balled up the cardigan and stuffed it between her leg and the side of the chair. Straightening her back, she rolled her shoulders and asked, "So, what do you want to know?"

RJ lifted the left side of her mouth in a sympathetic smile. "Tell me about him. For now, just tell me about James."

Janice sniffed, and a squeak escaped from her lips. RJ feared she would lose control again but she held herself together and, for the first time, looked RJ directly in the eye.

"He's . . . he was a wonderful man. We met at college, before he made his money. I didn't give him a second look when he asked me out the first time, but he pursued me relentlessly. To some, it might have seemed obsessive, but James . . . well, once he had his mind set on something, he didn't stop until he got what he'd set out to achieve. He worked hard all his life, whether he was making money or giving it away. And he did a lot of that. Gave money away, I mean. He knew what it was like to have it tough and wanted to give others a helping hand. I don't really know what else to tell you." She looked up at RJ. "My family wasn't pleased when I agreed to marry him. They soon changed their tune once he made those first millions only months later. Snobs, the lot of them, even Michael. Didn't seem to matter when he needed campaign funds, though, did it?"

"Did your family get along with James before his death?"

Janice raised her hands to her face and rubbed them over her cheeks, pulling the skin up at her ears like a grotesque facelift. "They all love him now. Loved him, I mean. I still can't get used to saying that. They started loving him as soon as they realized he was going to be wildly successful and rich. Congratulated me on our pairing, can you believe that? James didn't care, though. He was too kind-hearted to think badly of anyone. He even justified their attitudes to me. If he had any faults, it was that he was too understanding, too nice. Don't get me wrong, James was a hard ass in the boardroom, but he cared about people. That's what first attracted me to him. He was driven and had to be the best at everything. He had to be the king of the jungle, but he was kind to people. He always was."

She stared out over the lake and swallowed.

"What about your social life, your friends?"

"James was too busy for all that. He worked and came home and only attended necessary engagements—charity dinners or political events. That's all he had time for. Work. We went on vacation a couple of times a year, and he went hunting."

"Did you ever go with him? Hunting, I mean?"

"God forbid! That's not really my thing. He tried to get me interested a few times but no such luck. Sometimes I'd tag along on a trip, but it was good for him to be on his own sometimes. I pretty much left him to it. He was constantly surrounded by work and people—everyone was always demanding his time, for work or whatever his latest project was. He needed some alone time, some time to focus on something else."

"And you didn't go to Scotland with him?"

"No. Not this time." Tears started to slide down Janice's already streaked cheeks.

"Did James—or you, for that matter—receive any threats? Did anything suspicious happen recently, anything that might now seem suspicious?"

"No. I'm not sure if he'd have told me anyway, but nothing that I know of. No. Nothing. I don't believe he was murdered. I know Michael is concerned, but I'm not. Even if he was . . . It makes no difference."

"It makes a difference," replied RJ softly.

"Not to me. He's still dead. Whatever happened to him . . . nothing's going to bring him back." Janice slumped back into the chair, covered her face with her hands, and sobbed. "Michael's just,

Michael's just . . ." She shook her head, then took some long, deep breaths. "He wants me to see a doctor, get some pharmaceutical help. I don't want to be numb. I need . . . I don't know what I need. I just need James."

Rapid, shaking breaths threatened to overcome her.

"Michael wants to run for president in seven years. Did you know? He's worried someone was blackmailing James and that it could ruin his precious reputation and his chances of running. I know he's worried about me, but that's the real reason he hired you. He doesn't realize that I know, but I do. James would have been Michael's biggest backer. It's all just . . . just . . ." She threw her arms up in an act of futility.

"Do you think someone could have killed James to get to Michael?"

"No. Anything's possible, but I don't believe so. There are easier ways to get to Michael than through James. It doesn't make any sense. None of it makes any sense. I feel like I'm in a nightmare I can't wake up from. I keep expecting him to walk in the door." She looked up to the sky, tears brimming over her eyes before she jumped up and walked to the edge of the jetty. She leaned on the guard rail, her tears dripping into the water below.

RJ waited until Janice turned to face her. "When was the last time you spoke to James?"

"The police came around on the morning of Friday the seventeenth. I spoke to him the previous morning, just before lunch, my time. He'd had a good day. Just finished a tour of the estate where he was hunting. He was so excited to go out the next day to get started, and kept going on about the food on the menu that night. Every dish was caught or had been grown on the estate. He was like a kid in a candy store. He was having a good time."

"He wasn't worried about anything, bothered by something?"

"No, just the opposite. If you're going to ask, or are asking in a roundabout way, if I think he might have killed himself, then the answer is no. He had plans—*we* had plans. He just wouldn't. If there was anyone who wouldn't, it was him. If you knew him, you'd know he just wouldn't." She looked at RJ with such a ferocity in her eyes that RJ believed her, or at least, believed that Janice had faith in what she was saying. "I realize that everyone always says that, but I know him. He just wouldn't. He had what some might say was an unyielding spirit. If there was a problem or an issue, he would find the solution, no matter what. He always had to be in control. Even if he didn't have the answer to something, he was always confident that he would find it. It's the reason we have all of this." Janice gestured dismissively at the house, her face screwed up in pain. "He was excited about some new challenges and opportunities ahead. He would not do what you're suggesting."

"Okay," RJ reassured her in a soothing voice. "I had to ask, so we can rule it out."

"His boat was due to be put in the water tomorrow. It would have sat right there." Janice pointed just to the left of RJ's seat. "He would've been out on it first thing in the morning, trying to catch the monster bass that supposedly lives in the lake. No one we know has ever caught it. It's always been someone who knew someone who knew someone else who caught it. They all believed in it, all the fishermen round here. It can get quite competitive in the summer. James was determined to be the one who finally caught it. He won't get that chance now." She dissolved into another fit of sobbing.

RJ stood up and laid her hand on Janice's shoulder.

"I have to ask, and I apologize in advance, but have you ever had any reason to suspect that your husband was unfaithful?"

Janice looked at her with pure hatred. "How . . . you can't seriously think—"

RJ tried to look conciliatory but offered no further comment.

Janice put her chin up and through clenched teeth, replied, "James would never cheat on me, nor I him. We loved each other. You have no idea."

RJ was getting nowhere fast and it was clear that she'd get no further with Janice Sullivan in her current state. She thanked her for her time and told her she would be in touch as she handed over her card and asked her to call if she thought of anything else that might help the investigation. "Nothing is insignificant, no piece of information is too small."

Janice radiated a quiet rage as RJ prepared her retreat.

"I'm so sorry for your loss, Mrs. Sullivan," she said before making her way back down the jetty towards the house, her car and, ultimately, a small village near the Highlands of Scotland.

Chapter 4

RJ looked out at the landscape below as the plane circled, waiting for permission to land. Green fields and craggy peaks gave way to industrial estates and high-density housing. Motorways filled with ant-like cars snaked through the land, filling her field of vision as the plane tipped slightly to the side. She felt nothing. She hadn't been sure what she had expected to feel, but from this height, this land felt as alien to her now as the Sahara Desert. It was no longer home—her parents' deaths had ensured that it never would be again. It didn't fill her with the same dread she'd felt when she had to leave it before, when she escaped to the other side of the Atlantic to take up her professorship in what was now another world away.

No, she didn't feel dread. She tried to pinpoint what she was feeling but came up empty. Nothing, she felt nothing.

Even though she'd assured her uncle that she would be fine, she herself had been worried about her reaction to being back in Scotland. As it didn't seem to have the effect on her that she had feared, she felt ready to hit the ground running. She'd managed some sleep on the flight and had spent the rest of her time going over the facts as she knew them. Which, at the moment, weren't much.

James Sullivan, self-made tech billionaire, forty-three. Married to wife Janice for twenty-one years, no children. Workaholic. Brother-in-law to Governor Michael Kowalski, who had lofty plans to enter the presidential race. Philanthropist. Brought up on the wrong side of the tracks. Keen hunter. No known enemies.

Not much to go on. She hoped her assignment partner, whoever he was, would know more by the time she landed. All she knew about her partner was that he was from the UK branch of Kingfisher and was scheduled to meet her in the Arrivals hall, then drive her up to the area where James Sullivan's death had occurred.

RJ squirmed in her seat, unable to sit still. She was itching to start work. The plane seemed to circle for an age before the captain announced, "Cabin crew, please take your seats for landing," in that generic voice that belonged to pilots all over the world.

She continued to watch the once-familiar world below her become more real as they descended. The plane straightened, a grinding noise indicating the wheels had been lowered. RJ's stomach flipped as the plane dropped lower. Her stomach flipped again when the wheels finally touched down and the passengers were thrown forward slightly due to the forward momentum. One person gave a solitary, congratulatory clap to the captain as the plane began to slow.

The lines for immigration moved quickly, and RJ's bag was one of the first to come through, so she didn't have time to think before she stepped through the double doors and into Arrivals. She'd been told her partner would have a sign with the name Fisher on it. She scanned the waiting crowd, dismissing those people obviously looking for family members until she found the small group of drivers and tour guides, no doubt waiting for golfers or history buffs keen to discover what Scotland had to offer them in way of sport, culture, and probably more than a little whisky.

Seeing no sign, she scanned the hall again but still no luck. She walked towards the tour guides and almost walked past one leaning nonchalantly against a pillar. His sign read Urquhart Tours but on closer look she saw his name badge displayed the name T. Fisher.

"I believe you're looking for me," she said as she looked up to meet his eyes.

"That'll be right," he said and turned sharply on his heel, his earlier lassitude seemingly forgotten. He moved quickly but favored one leg over the other. He was either trying to hide his limp or it was an old injury. There was no way someone with a recent injury could move that fast.

RJ followed, more than a little annoyed. She struggled to keep up with him as he weaved in and out of the crowd. Hampered by her large bag, she dodged and swerved around travelers and their companions. When they emerged into the dull afternoon light and crossed the street to the car park, he didn't slow his pace at all, remaining a step ahead of her the entire time.

She followed him to an old silver Saab. He got in at the driver's side, popping the boot as he did so.

RJ looked on in disbelief at the man she was to spend her time with on this assignment, took a deep breath, and moved to the back of the car. She easily managed her bag but had to reorganize the existing contents in the boot to make room for her bag. She squeezed two black hold-alls deep into the boot and moved a small suitcase to the side, then slid her own in, pushing the top of the boot down with extra force to ensure it clicked shut.

"Look, I don't know what the problem is, but we'd better get it sorted out now," she told him as she climbed into the passenger side and closed the door.

"Really?" he asked, his face contorted with disdain.

"Whatever the issue is, we have to work together. We won't be able to do that very well if we can't even have a civil conversation."

"You really don't recognize me, do you?'

RJ studied his face. He did look ever so slightly familiar, but she just couldn't place him. Surely, she'd never have any reason to have met him . . .

Recognition hit her like a slap in the face. "Oh. Oh, I, um . . . oh." Heat rose to her cheeks as she realized where she knew him from. He looked very different from the rat-like man she'd met when she was unknowingly in the middle of her interview for Kingfisher. The rat-like man who had chased her through Hyde Park. The rat-like man whose kneecap she had shattered in an attempt to get away. "I . . . um. I didn't get the chance to say how sorry I am. I didn't know. I am so, so sorry"

RJ stared at her hands in her lap in mortification. She felt his eyes boring into her and looked up to meet them. He looked so different from the person she had met briefly in Hyde Park. Had he been wearing a prosthetic then, or was he simply able to change his demeanor in such a way as to look like a completely different character? The man in front of her now was not rat-like in any form. In actual fact, he was not unattractive. He would have been attractive if his gaze wasn't about to reduce RJ to a pile of ash and rubble. The slick-backed hair she had seen previously was now thick and wavy, the sleeves of his blue shirt pushed up past his elbows, and the khaki chinos could have fitted in any situation and with people from every walk of life. She couldn't determine his age, but due to the disarmingly attractive effect of laughter lines that had started to form around his eyes, she figured he was in his late-thirties.

"Not your fault, I suppose," he said begrudgingly. "You actually thought I was going to hurt you. I should've been better prepared. They should have told me you knew how to do that."

"They didn't know," she said, speaking of the organization they both worked for.

He scowled. "They know everything." Glancing over his shoulder, he pulled out into the lane that would take them over the Erskine Bridge to the other side of the River Clyde and Loch Lomond beyond.

RJ played with the ring on her right finger, twisting the smooth metal off and on over her knuckle.

They passed the next few minutes in awkward silence until RJ couldn't stand it anymore.

"Seems an odd choice, don't you think? To put us together for this after—"

"You'd already been assigned to the case," he told her in resignation. "I'm the most obvious partner available in the country as I've got mountain-climbing experience. We might need it up there. Putting us together makes sense to them. This is my first assignment since I got back from leave. Believe me, if I could have gotten out of it, I would have."

"You said you didn't blame me."

"I don't, but I'm under no obligation to enjoy the experience, either."

RJ sighed. "Noted."

The countryside whizzed past in direct contrast with the slow march of time within the car.

It was strange being back. Surreal. RJ had driven this road countless times on road trips with her family or with friends, and now she was back again. So much had changed for her since the last time she'd been on this road, yet this place had been frozen in time. It felt both like she'd never left and like her life there had never existed at all. It didn't feel like home anymore, just like a place where she used to live at one point in her life. If this wasn't home, then where was? Did she even have a home now?

Yes, she realized, her home was with Benjamin. Home was wherever her family was, and right now that consisted of Ben.

They slowed to a crawl behind a tractor, the traffic quickly building up behind them. A mile down the road, the tractor pulled off to the side and waved them past. They pulled over at the next rest stop to let the line of impatient traffic speed off to wherever they all had to be in such a hurry.

"So, what's our story?" RJ asked.

"We're Riley and Stuart Black. I'm older than you, obviously, by eight years. We met in Birmingham when you were a student. We used to get the same train into the city every day and sat beside each other for months before I plucked up the courage to talk to you. You're an artist, and I've just been made redundant from an advertising agency in London—our home for the past ten years. We're scouting out places to build or develop into an artist retreat. A new business venture, away from the rat race, and a way to invest my redundancy."

"Sounds plausible enough. So, we're married then. I should have guessed." RJ swapped the ring she'd been toying with over to her left hand.

"We're staying in the village near where Sullivan stayed. It's about ten miles outside Oban. Our booking is open-ended depending on how long it takes us to scout the area. I've spoken to the owner and described our situation. They seem to be glad of the length of the booking. Must be hard times. They were willing to accommodate us for as long as we needed."

"Any updates on the case?"

"What do you know so far?" he asked her.

She filled him in on all she knew as well as her visit to Janice Sullivan.

"We've had a lot more come through since you were last updated, it seems. They're still combing through the emails and texts of both the Sullivans and Kowalski. Nothing popped yet. No signs or rumors of any extra-marital activity on any side. The financials for his companies are panning out so far. None of his companies are in trouble. Looking into his past is proving to be a bit more problematic. He had a number of associates when he was younger that are now either dead or incarcerated. Statistically, it's no different than what we would expect from such a cohort. They're trying to see if there are any current links to his old friends, but nothing has surfaced yet. The biggest piece of information is that we now know who he transferred the money to."

"And who would that be?"

"Buchanan Estate, the place where he was staying and hunting."

"The payment makes sense, but why was the trail hidden so well? That's just odd."

"The payment wasn't for his room and board or his hunting privileges. That all went through the official company account." Stuart shook his head. "And the amount is higher than you'll have heard. We found more hidden payments from another of Sullivan's bank accounts. It totals fifty thousand dollars. There were no upcoming payments, but that doesn't mean he wasn't planning on paying them even more."

"Then just what was he paying them for? That money amounts to almost forty thousand pounds. And why was it put through separately?"

"All good questions that we still have to find the answers to."

They passed the rest of the drive in silence, with RJ mulling over the new information, and Stuart, or whatever his real name was, stewing in his own juices, sitting beside the woman who had inadvertently knee-capped him.

Chapter 6

Although she had visited the town of Oban many times before, RJ, like most people, had never ventured to the village of Ferlieclachan, which lay ten miles east of the main town. Hardly surprising since the village was not situated on any main roads. A reminder of its stark remoteness was that the country road which led to Ferlieclachan ran out of tarmac a few hundred yards from the village pub. It was at the pub that Stuart slowed down and pulled in.

"Home sweet home," he muttered under his breath as he pulled up the hand brake. "Wait here." He unclipped his seatbelt and exited the car, going in through the well-handled wooden doors of the old, whitewashed stone building.

RJ stared after him and chewed the inside of her cheek. They'd need to get over their issues if they were to masquerade as husband and wife. She'd talk to him this evening, try to clear the air. If they didn't hash it out now, then working together could get very unpleasant. A plan of action decided, she peered out the windscreen at the old building. It looked like it had been there since time began. Weeds jutted out where the stone blocks met the pavement, the stoop worn from the footsteps of probably hundreds of years of clientele. She looked up at the flaking black paint on the blocks surrounding the windows above. It didn't bode well, but then, she wasn't here for a holiday. A little round face suddenly appeared at the top window, disappearing out of sight as quickly as it had appeared. RJ was still watching the window for any further signs of life when Stuart got back in the car.

"We're to go 'round the side," he told her as he started the car and reversed out of the space.

They stopped at a metal gate covered in chicken wire that wouldn't have looked out of place on a farm. A woman with a frizzy, auburn mane and rosy cheeks marched up to the other side and swung it open for them. She waved them through with a friendly smile, then closed and fastened the gate behind them.

What awaited them on the property was a steep bank containing three black-and-white cabins painted to match the main building. Two large oak trees spread their branches and roots out between the cabins, their boughs towering over the roofs like ancient guardians and protectors. Beyond the property line, designated by a fence of the same ilk as the gate, was a thick pine-tree plantation, the entire sector at a forty-five-degree angle to the top left already harvested. Freshly cut stumps and the waste of the seized trees provided a desolate and alien backdrop to what was to be their home for the duration of the assignment.

The cabins rested on gravel-filled platforms set into the hill. Wooden staircases with no handrails led from each one to join a winding path that started at an empty area of hard standing, obviously designated as car parking.

The tires crunched as Stuart eased into the area the landlady was pointing to, leaving space on either side for other cars—should there be any.

"Lovely to have you here," the landlady said with a wide but tired smile as they got out of the car. "You're the only ones here, so you have your choice of cabins, but I thought I'd put you in number two. It's got the best views."

Her strong brogue was a sudden reminder to RJ of exactly where she was. It was jarring to hear the accent after so long and sounded alien after the time she had spent away. She gave herself a mental shake and resigned herself to the fact that she'd be hearing a lot more of it on this assignment. She just had to tune in and get used to it again.

"Sound's lovely, doesn't it, darling?" Stuart turned to RJ with a smile and took her hand in his.

RJ plastered a grin on her face.

As they followed their host up the stairs, RJ noted that she was wearing long sleeves even though it was a relatively warm evening. She could have kicked herself—she'd completely forgotten about midges. She hated the little buggers, and now she would have to deal with the constant itching that Highland summers provided.

"Oh, I never introduced myself, I'm Tracy," she told them as she put the key in the door.

Tracy's clothes were worn. They were undoubtedly clean but had clearly seen better days. Jeans that had once been black were a washed out-gray, and the plaid shirt she wore over a vest had a thin layer of light fuzz covering it in its entirety. The running shoes she wore were scuffed and discolored.

Tracy turned the handle, but the door wouldn't budge. Putting her shoulder against the wood, she pushed, turning the handle at the same time. "Just needs a wee shove," she explained as she grunted with an effort that was rewarded with an open door. "If you need anything at all, you just let me know."

She waited in the doorway as they took in the cabin in all its splendor. There was one main room, with a window facing the front. A double bed had been pushed against the back wall, with a sofa in front of the window and small kitchen area to one side. A door off the kitchen presumably led to the bathroom. The cabin smelled musty, like it needed a good airing out, but appeared clean and tidy, even if the furniture did look a bit worse for wear and the carpet was worn away to within an inch of its life. If this was the best cabin, RJ wondered what the other choices provided.

"It's great, just what we need," she reassured Tracy.

"Yep, perfect," Stuart added. "A great little base."

"So, you folks are looking for property, eh?"

"Yes, yes, we are. This is the perfect spot for us to stay while we're looking. If you've any leads, please let us know. Maybe you could put the word out in the pub for us?" Stuart suggested.

"I'll certainly ask around." Tracy beamed. "I haven't heard of anything, to be honest. Usually someone would have to die with no family for the sort of thing you're looking for to come up around here." She offered them an apologetic smile, her cheeks flushing a deeper shade of red.

"Not that I want to put you off, what would I know?" She shrugged. "Breakfast is served in the pub at seven-thirty if you want to book ahead."

"Oh, I think we'll be fine sorting our own out," Stuart said. "Although, I'm sure we'll see you in the pub at the end of a long day's property search."

"Well, I'll be seeing you. If there's anything you need, just give me a shout. Oh, and those wee nyaffs that you'll see around, they'll be mine."

"Nyaffs?"

"Aye, my weans, I've got three of them. Twin boys and a girl."

RJ thought of the little face she'd seen at the widow, no doubt one of Tracy's kids curious about their new visitors.

"A nyaff is an annoying person, darling," RJ explained to her 'husband' with a forced smile and an emphasis on the word 'darling'.

Tracy was either oblivious to RJ's dig towards Stuart or too polite to indicate that she'd noticed. RJ bet it was the first option. Tracy, it seemed, had enough on her plate without worrying about the personal life of her guests.

"Anyways, if they're any bother, let me know."

"Oh, I'm sure we'll be fine." RJ smiled, understanding why Tracy had dark circles beneath her eyes. "Thank you."

Tracy retreated down the stairs and RJ shut the door, shoving it back in place with her shoulder.

"There really wasn't much choice in the way of accommodation round here," Stuart said as she turned around. "However, we couldn't get much closer to the estate than this. Those trees at the back are on Buchanan land, and the main gate is just down the road." He walked over to the window and pushed it open. "Get this place aired out in no time."

"I'm sure it'll be fine. Just like camping." Hands on her hips, she looked around and considered the space, her eyes coming to rest on the bed in the corner.

Stuart smirked at her.

She glared at him. "There's no way we're sharing."

"If that's the case, you'll need to take the couch," he said. "Look at the size of me compared to you. Plus, I need to be able to stretch out my knee," he added with a malicious grin.

He was at least a full head and neck taller than she was, and he did have a point about his knee, although she hoped he'd drop it soon or they'd never be able to work together.

"Fine by me."

She turned back around, planting her feet firmly as she struggled to pull the door open. When it finally budged, she stepped outside to get her bag from the car. On her way down the steps, she noticed she had an audience—that same little face that had been spying on her from the upstairs window. The girl, who looked to be about five or six, sat upon a rusty swing-set in the corner of the lot, staring at RJ just as intently as before. This time, though, she had no place to retreat to when RJ caught her eye.

"Hello," RJ called in greeting and lifted her hand.

The girl lifted her hand to wave back. There was a moment's hesitation before she hopped off the swing and ambled over to where RJ was now trying to pull her hold-all out of the car. She pushed strands of hair the same color as her mother's away from her face and peered up at RJ, eyes filled with curiosity.

"Is it just you?" the little girl asked her.

"Just me?"

"Got any kids with you?" she asked hopefully.

"No, sorry, just me and my husband." RJ pitied the little mite. There didn't seem to be a lot to do around here at first glance.

"You've got a ton o' stuff fir just two people," she said as she peered at all the bags stuffed into the small boot.

"Yeah, actually we do," RJ agreed, looking at the contents of the car in consternation. No way was she going to lug all of it up to the cabin. Stuart better get his butt into gear. If she had to sleep on the couch, he could carry his own bags.

Suddenly, something rubbed up against her leg. She let out a sharp gasp, relieved when she looked down to see a tortoiseshell cat trying to wind itself round her ankles.

"That's Socks. He loves everybody. Don't you, Socks? My name's Kirsty."

Socks meowed up at RJ. She bent to run her hands over his soft fur. "A very good name," she said as she looked at the little white paws trying to clamber onto her lap. She laughed and stood up again, much to the cat's chagrin. His incessant meowing voiced his frustration.

RJ smiled down at the little girl and held out her hand.

Kirsty looked at RJ's hand, then up at her face, before looking down again and placing her hand carefully in RJ's and shaking it. She seemed unsure of herself, and RJ deduced it was the first time she'd ever performed the grown-up ritual with anyone.

"It's very nice to meet you, Kirsty. I hope we can be friends even if I'm not quite the age you were hoping for."

Kirsty gathered herself up to her full height. "Nice . . . to meet you, too, missus," she said, trying out the unfamiliar words.

"You can call me Riley," RJ said.

"Uh . . . okay."

"Your mum said you had brothers," RJ prompted as Kirsty stood and watched her struggle to pull her bag free from its tightly wedged place.

"Aye," Kirsty said as she picked up the cat and cradled it in her arms. The cat went along with the process as if resigned to its fate. "But they hardly ever want to play with me. They say am too wee."

"Brothers, eh?" RJ shut the boot and picked up her bag. She was surprised to see the cat purring contentedly in Kirsty's arms—clearly, she had been wrong about his displeasure. "It looks like someone else appreciates you very much," RJ said, tilting her head towards the happy cat.

Kirsty grinned at the cat, then graced RJ with that toothy grin. "Aye, Socks is a right wee sook. He loves cuddles. I'm his favorite," she announced proudly. "The boys don't really do cuddles." She screwed up her face and rolled her eyes, looking every bit like a teenager trapped in a five-year-old's body.

RJ rolled her eyes in solidarity. "Well, Socks is lucky to have you to give him plenty of cuddles."

"Kirsty!" Tracy's voice rang out over the grounds. "Tea!"

The little girl turned on her heel and ran in the direction of the back door of the pub, the poor cat jostling in her arms.

"Cheerio, missus," she shouted over her shoulder before she disappeared into the pub.

RJ smiled at the spot where Kirsty had stood, then swung the hold-all over her shoulder and trudged back up the steps to the bundle of laughs that was Stuart.

He better get over himself quick, RJ thought as she put her shoulder to the door and pushed. She found him standing in the middle of the room, signing off with whomever he had just been talking to on the phone.

"There's been a development," Stuart told her as he put away his phone, his earlier annoyance with her seemingly forgotten. He waited until RJ had closed the door. "We've just found out that James Sullivan wasn't the first to die at the estate. The same procurator fiscal was involved in the investigation, or rather lack of investigation, of both deaths. This isn't an isolated incident. We'll need to tread carefully."

Chapter 7

"What do you mean? Who else died?"

"A gamekeeper, two years ago. Name was David MacKay. Took his own life, supposedly."

"On the estate?"

"On the estate," he confirmed. "Closed casket, due to the nature of his injuries. Shotgun to the head."

"Do we think it's related to the Sullivan death?" RJ asked. "It makes sense that the same fiscal dealt with the case. It's in the same area. He would deal with all sudden-death cases here. It might just be a coincidence." She paced in the small area between the door and the kitchen as she digested the information.

"Something tells me not." He shrugged. "Call it a gut instinct. A bit of free advice—when you've been in this game as long as I have, you learn to listen to your gut."

She stopped pacing mid-step and whirled round to face him, her jaw set in a hard line. "Don't patronize me. I may be relatively new to the organization, but I'm not stupid. Just because I have a lot to learn doesn't mean I'm thick. If you treat me as if I am, we aren't going to get very far."

They stared at each other, expressionless, each unwilling to give anything away. RJ was the first to break the silence. If she didn't, they'd be stuck in that stalemate all night. She took a breath and calmed herself, conscious that she was just as responsible for the success of their relationship as he was.

"How long have you been in this game?" she asked him, putting as much sincerity into her tone as she could muster.

Stuart let out a loud sigh, and RJ could see some of the tension ease from his shoulders. It was about time he realized that they couldn't be at loggerheads the entire time they had to work together. And who knew how long that would be?

"Fifteen years, give or take. They recruited me straight after I'd left the army."

RJ looked at the man in front of her with newfound admiration. "Is that where they get most of us, from the services?"

"Well, they don't routinely recruit geologists, if that's what you mean."

RJ ignored the dig at her previous occupation.

"It makes a lot of sense to recruit from the armed forces," Stuart continued. "We can stay calm under pressure and know how to survive."

She nodded. "So, what's the plan now?"

"I think the first thing we should do tomorrow is go for a walk on the estate. Do a bit of recon. Hang on." He went out to the car, returning a few moments later with a bag in each hand and one over his shoulder. He set them down and rummaged in the largest one, taking out binoculars, wet-bags filled with something soft, and a crumpled, waxed map which he laid out on the small dining table. He motioned with his hand for her to join him.

As they sat hunched over the map, he pointed out their current location. "Look here. Where the road ends, that's the entrance to the estate. All this that's ringed in red is the Buchanan Estate. All hundred-and-fifty-three thousand acres of it."

"Jeez." RJ marveled at the scope and size of the land. It covered the mountains to the east, forests, farmland, rivers, and streams. It swept down and under the town of Oban in a wide curve, claiming all that fell in its path. "It's huge," she muttered. "Where do we start?"

"We can assume they all went in the front door, so to speak, so we'll start there. We'd better get a good night's sleep. Tomorrow is going to be a long day of hiking."

The couch, which had been perfectly fine to sit on, morphed into a mass of lumps and bumps when RJ tried to settle down to sleep. Even though it was designed for two people to sit comfortably and she was much shorter than Stuart, she had to curl up uncomfortably to fit. She tossed and turned, unable to find a position that would afford her any rest. Eventually she stood up, glaring at Stuart's snoring form in the bed. She pulled the seat cushions off the couch, berated herself for not having done so before, then pushed the coffee table closer to the window and wedged the cushions between the table and couch. Flopping down contentedly, with her feet hanging over the edge of the cushions, she fell asleep almost instantly. It felt like she'd only been asleep for minutes when she awoke to the unwelcome sounds of Stuart clattering around in the small kitchenette.

Raising her bedraggled head, she peered at Stuart out of one eye. "What time is it?"

"Five forty-five," he informed her. "We need to get a jump on the day. Here." He handed her a bowl of mush that at one time might have been called muesli.

RJ wrinkled her nose in disgust. "What is it?"

"Breakfast. The rest of the day's ration packs are in our day packs."

"Ration packs? We're going for a hike, not advancing on enemy insurgents in the desert."

"We'll get the calories we need without the added weight in our packs."

RJ buried her face in her pillow in resignation and screamed into the mound of feathers. The fact that Stuart made so much sense infuriated her. Her first assignment had instilled a firm sense of confidence in her. She had been the sole agent protecting Ted Jamison and had been perfectly capable of the task, both physically and intellectually. She'd received a glowing report for her efforts from Ted and then from her uncle, the director of Kingfisher. Even her interview had given her confidence. She'd dealt with everything they had thrown at her from getting shot at, to overseas travel to London, to hunting down and infiltrating the organization that had put her through the ringer. Her, so far, short experience with Kingfisher, combined with her training, had ensured that she felt ready, comfortable in her new skin as what, in effect, was a secret agent. Being paired with Stuart, however, upset that equilibrium. He was sarcastic, mean, and unforgiving of their earlier altercation, but he was so much more suited to the task at hand than RJ was. His experience made her feel like an incompetent child. What the hell use was she going to be on a countryside reconnaissance?

She lifted her head, inhaling and exhaling deeply, calming her mind and giving herself a mental shake. She had something to give this case. So, what if he was well prepared? She flourished at the unexpected.

Learn from the man and his experience. And learn from yourself, too.

She sat up with her back against the couch and spooned a lump of the mush into her mouth, chewing cautiously. "Not as bad as it looks," she admitted. "But promise me we'll go to the pub for breakfast tomorrow."

"Sure, whatever." He rolled his eyes, and RJ could see his patience with her beginning to wane over her greenness.

RJ's blood began to simmer. Taking a breath to steady herself, she put the bowl down and held her hands up in a gesture of supplication. "We need to work together on this. I'm truly sorry for what happened to your knee—"

"You happened to my knee."

"Yes, well . . . We've already been over that. Look, we've got very different backgrounds and styles of work. Presumably that's why we were made partners on this. Let's use those differences to our advantage instead of allowing them to create problems." God, this guy infuriated her.

"I agree."

"You do?" She narrowed her eyes in suspicion at his sudden attitude change.

"We've got a job to do. Let's just get on with it. Never mind the rest of this crap." Though he waved her off, his biting tone and stiff shoulders negated his words.

RJ's attempt at clearing the air only increased their frustration. When they closed the door behind them, they were no closer to liking each other than they had been when RJ had climbed into Stuart's car the day before. They had, however, called an unspoken truce.

They left the car in its spot and followed the road to the estate's entrance. Miles of wire fences culminated in an oddball of an entrance. Two stone pillars shaped like turrets rose from a short wall that grew incongruously from the grass. A cast-iron sign on the closed gate read *Private Property*. A painted metal banner between the turrets with the name *Buchanan* emblazoned across a coat of arms of a lion rampant beneath an ornate helmet and crown completed the look. A metal road led from the gate far into the depths of the estate.

"It doesn't look like they welcome unexpected visitors." RJ turned to look at Stuart. Her partner was bent over with one leg through the fence, his arm outstretched to hold the fence wire up above his head.

"No, it doesn't," he agreed, straightening on the other side of the fence.

RJ handed him her pack and slipped through the fence.

It felt like she'd stepped into the lion's den, and the lion rampant on the crest flashed through her mind like a bad omen.

Stuart tilted his head, his eyes asking whether she was ready. She nodded, and they headed towards the cover of the pine trees a few hundred yards to the left.

Once they reached the forest, RJ felt a lot less exposed. Trespassing made her uneasy. Even though, legally, they had a right to roam over most of Scotland, she didn't imagine this would end well—especially not if the landowners were trying to cover up suspicious deaths.

"Come on," Stuart urged her. "We've got a lot of ground to cover."

RJ quickened her pace, inhaling the fresh scent of pine needles, letting it fill her lungs and ease her anxiety. She hopped over a fallen bough, the dropped needles crunching under her boots as she landed on the soft brown cover. Keeping her partner in sight, she tried to see through the mass of trees to the clearing ahead. It proved impossible. No matter which way she turned, she could only see a world that consisted of trees and their detritus. She doubted she would be able to find her way out without the compass on her company phone and the spare map Stuart had packed in her bag in case something happened and they got separated.

An hour later, RJ finally spotted a way out of the trees. No sooner had she seen the glimmer of open space than they emerged into the blinding light of morning sun that was still low in the sky. They breached another fence and set off across a field liberally sprinkled with fresh sheep droppings, though there were no sheep in sight. They were careful to avoid stepping in the gifts of olfactory unpleasantness, not through any sense of squeamishness but for fear of leaving evidence of their own presence.

A stream gurgled nearby, and as they reached it, it became evident that they would need to cross it. Stuart leapt over it, but since RJ didn't have the same length of stride, she had to move further down the slight slope in hopes of finding a narrower point to cross. As she came over a small rise, she stopped in her tracks. She retched, the mush she'd had for breakfast threatening to rise, but she swallowed it down and took a steadying breath through her mouth. A sheep lay splayed out before her, its entrails ripped from its stomach, the stench of blood ripe in the air. She knelt to examine the damage more closely, but she couldn't tell if anything was missing or if the unfortunate animal still had all its body parts. Flies buzzed around the corpse, hampering her examination.

"What happened to it?" Stuart asked from the other side of the stream.

"Not sure. But it's not been dead long. No maggots," RJ explained without looking up.

"Wolves?"

"There are no wolves in Scotland. Some landowners are trying to get them brought from Scandinavia and the like to help keep the deer numbers down, but nothing's happened yet."

"You sure about that?" he asked.

"Hmm." She took a minute to look up at the sky. "Could be a number of things. Natural death, after which an eagle or hawk perhaps got hold of her. Whatever got her, it had to be sharp enough to slit her open. Can you think of any reason a farmer might do that?"

"No, but that doesn't mean they didn't. Let's get out of here." He looked around uneasily. "Whatever this is, I don't like it."

RJ stood up and looked at him across the water. "Agreed."

A rock that had been rubbed smooth by the constant flow of water jutted out in the middle of the stream. Gingerly, she placed her foot on the rock, then leapt over to the opposite bank.

After one last look at the eviscerated ewe, the pair swiftly walked away.

Twenty minutes later, Stuart slowed to a stop to check his map. "We need to head up there." He pointed to a ridge that rose steeply from the rolling hillside. "That's where Sullivan supposedly fell."

A rumble in the distance made them turn and look down to the valley below. Far beneath them, a car could be seen headed in their direction. As it got closer, the car solidified into an old Land Rover that seemed to be held together by the layers of mud that covered it.

"Keep walking," Stuart urged her.

"But it's heading right for us."

"You're right." Reluctantly, he stopped to wait for its arrival. It wasn't long before the car rolled up in front of them, its window down, the occupant a gnarled-looking man in his fifties with an expression as cold as ice.

"You're on private property."

RJ gave him her biggest smile. "Sorry, we didn't realize. Just out for the day, exploring."

"You'd have had to go over a fence to get in here." His face was impassive with deep crevices carved into his forehead. Whether this was due to exposure on the job or a hard life was impossible to say, most likely it was both. He got out of the car, his wax jacket over a checked shirt and jeans looking far too uncomfortable and hot for the warm weather. Wisps of gray hair poked out from under a flat cap that had seen better days.

Stuart ignored the man's attempt at intimidation. "Lovely day for it. We're considering buying property in the area. Figured we'd look round a bit."

"There's nothin' for sale up round here. All this . . ." He gestured with both hands. "Buchanan land."

"Are you Mr. Buchanan?" RJ enquired in a syrupy tone.

The man looked at her as if she'd just mortally insulted him, or mortally insulted Mr. Buchanan—she couldn't tell which.

"I'm the gamekeeper. An' you need to leave."

Stuart narrowed his eyes. "You can't just chuck us off. What about right to roam?"

The gamekeeper blinked once and raised his eyes to the sky, taking in a lungful of country air. He'd obviously heard the argument more than once before. "That may be, but we have a rogue stag. Been trying to catch him for the last few months. This here's a dangerous place to be just now."

RJ looked out over the landscape below. All she could see was grass, rocks, and the flock of sheep that must've been in the previous field moving towards higher ground on a rocky ridge that would have caused trouble to any other animal. She looked up at the ridge on the opposite side, the one they had been trying to reach.

"Seems as though visibility is pretty good up here. I'm sure we'd be fine. You needn't to worry about us."

"You might think you can see everything up here, but you can't. That old bugger can come out of nowhere fast. You wouldn't know he was there till he'd gored you in the stomach."

The image of the dead sheep they'd encountered flashed through RJ's mind. She shuddered. If that was the handiwork of a large deer, she wouldn't want to suffer the same fate.

"'sides," he continued. "As I explained, we've been trying to get him for weeks. There's a permanent hunt on for him. If the deer doesn't get you, then the crossbows and rifles might." He looked pointedly at them, letting the information sink in. The man was certainly good at dramatics.

"Is that so?" said Stuart. It was clear that he was keen to show he wasn't cowed by the threat.

The men stared each other down—the gamekeeper leaning on the bonnet of his car, not giving an inch; Stuart, raising himself up to his full height, his neck flushed and a vein throbbing in his temple. He was like a tightly coiled spring set to explode.

Although the guy had threatened them, this posturing Stuart was doing would lead to no good in terms of their investigation. Surely, he realized that? The guy had clearly pushed Stuart's buttons for some reason, or perhaps that was what Stuart wanted the guy to believe?

As they waited for the other to concede defeat, RJ jumped in. "Well, now, it doesn't sound like our walk would be as relaxing as we intended, does it, darling?"

Her words and tone seemed to break through the tension inside Stuart. His shoulders visibly dropped, but his gaze remained on the gamekeeper. "No, I don't suppose we will. We'll get out of your hair and just head back the way we came," he told the gamekeeper.

"I'm afraid I can't allow that."

When nothing but silence followed his words, RJ wondered if Stuart could keep himself contained for much longer.

"Like I said, it's not safe. I'll drive you back. Make sure you get off the property in one piece. Last thing we need is the bad publicity of having some city tourists getting killed on the estate."

"Much obliged," Stuart said through clenched teeth. "But we didn't say we were from the city."

The gamekeeper sneered as he looked Stuart up and down. "You didn't have to."

He pushed off the car and got in. RJ and Stuart shared a glance. Seeing no other choice but to get in the car, RJ walked around to the passenger side while Stuart got in the back right behind the driver. RJ shifted a pile of newspapers from the seat to the floor and climbed in. An empty bottle of whisky rolled against her foot, and she wedged it between her leg and the door, within easy reaching distance. It could prove to be an effective weapon, if necessary.

"Belts," the man ordered, making no move to start the engine.

They clicked the seatbelts into place, and he turned the key, igniting the engine with a sputtering rumble.

"It's not exactly a smooth ride," he informed them. When he took off, they soon found out he wasn't exaggerating. The suspension on the old car was shot and they jostled about, banging from side to side. At one point, Stuart cursed as his head connected with the roof of the car. RJ's small stature was an advantage in their current situation.

"So," she said, keen to gather as much information as she could. "You mentioned dead tourists being bad publicity . . ."

"Aye."

"Am I right in thinking that this is where that American billionaire was killed?"

The squeak of the ineffective suspension and their own bodies being thrown around the small space was the only sound for the next few seconds.

"Aye . . ." he finally said.

"What was it that happened to him?" RJ asked innocently.

He turned to look at her, his eyes leaving the bumpy terrain. The look he shot her wasn't threatening, but it wasn't friendly, either. She swallowed as she waited for him to reply.

From the corner of her eye, RJ noticed Stuart move forward in his seat as if ready to attack from behind. Her hand found the neck of the empty bottle and she gripped it in preparation.

"An accident." His eyes clouded over with something RJ couldn't quite place as he looked back at the road again. "A terrible accident." He stopped for a beat. "I found him." The words were barely audible over the squeak of the suspension.

RJ loosened her grip and looked at the man with fresh sympathy. "I'm sorry. Sometimes it's easy to forget there are other lives involved in the stories we hear on the news." She placed her hand on his arm, and he turned his head to look at where she touched him as if her hand was burning through the heavy layers of his clothes. When he glanced back up into her eyes, RJ saw a man worn down by an unspeakable burden. There was a glimmer of fear deep down in there that was impossible to feign. Just what was he so afraid of? Suddenly, the moment was broken when he shifted into a lower gear to aid their passage down a particularly steep incline.

RJ withdrew and folded her hands in her lap as she considered his reaction.

The back of the car flew into the air as it reached the bottom of the incline. RJ was jostled out of her thoughts for the split-second that they were airborne, then they landed with a thump and another curse from Stuart. A short journey over a muddy field found them on the metal road that they had seen upon entering the estate. Now that they were on flat ground, the ride became smoother, and within minutes, they were back at the gates where they had started.

The gamekeeper got out and unlocked the formidable iron structure with a key from a heavy chain. He swung one side open with a deep squeak, the hinges desperate for a quenching drench in oil.

He held it open and ushered them through. "Don't come back on the estate again. It's not safe."

"We won't," RJ assured him. "Don't worry about us, we won't make that mistake again, will we, darling?" she asked her 'husband'.

"You know me, darling, I never make the same mistake twice," he said with a tight smile, then turned to the gamekeeper. "Thanks for seeing us back."

The man ignored him as he locked the gate and returned to the Land Rover.

They stood and watched as he turned the car around and headed back up the road. The minute they'd stepped through the gate, they had ceased to exist for him, his gaze never landing on them as he went back to wherever he had come from. It was difficult to fathom whether this physical evidence lay in direct contradiction to whatever was going on in his head. They had certainly raised suspicions with their presence.

Well, there wasn't much they could do about that now.

They turned around and started the short walk back to the pub and their cabin.

"Did you see how rattled he was when I mentioned Sullivan?"

"I did. Easily explained if he did find him after a fall, though. I've seen plenty of fatal injuries, none of them easy to get over. If he found him with his skull bashed in like the death certificate suggested, then—"

"If it had been only an accident, he wouldn't have been so keen to get us off the estate."

"What, you don't buy the story about the stag?" Stuart asked.

"No, do you?"

"I don't."

"They're hiding something up there that they don't want anyone to know about."

"It's a pretty big place to hide something. It'd be like searching for a needle in a haystack if we went back."

RJ shook her head. "If it was like looking for a needle in a haystack, then he wouldn't have been as keen to see us off. We'd never have just stumbled across whatever it is. No, this is something different. Something obvious." RJ racked her brain as she walked, matching her pace with Stuart's long strides.

"The employee who died . . . Surely if they had any problems with him, they'd just fire him. Why would they kill him? They wouldn't go to such efforts for an employee; they'd just get rid of them."

Mulling it over, she scratched at a red midge bite that appeared on her arm in a sudden itch. She hadn't noticed any while they were out but they must have kicked some up from the long grass. "What do we know about the land owner?"

"Jeffrey Buchanan, land's been in the family for hundreds of years. Clean as a whistle, no criminal history, nothing notable about the guy at all."

"Not having a record doesn't prove anything. He's got enough money to get away with a lot of things—maybe even murder."

"There are no links between him and Sullivan, we've checked," Stuart said.

"There must be something. Sullivan wouldn't have transferred all that money for nothing. There's something there. We just aren't seeing it."

"Well, I don't think we're going to come up with anything by trying to get on the estate again. We'll need to come up with another way in."

They reached the gate at the side of the pub, and RJ looped her hand over to lift the latch, pulling it open just enough for them to pass through. As they walked in, they saw two little boys, mirror images of one another, clambering up the furthest oak tree at the back of the property near the fence. Kirsty was scrambling at the bottom, trying—and failing—to find her way up. She was too short to reach the bough the boys must have used to pull themselves up into the higher branches.

"You're too wee, away and play with your dollies," one of the boys shouted.

"Silly, wee girl," shouted the other.

Dejected, Kirsty turned and walked back in the direction of her home. As she neared RJ and Stuart, they noticed her eyes brimming with tears. The girl put her head down in embarrassment, lifting her hand as she passed them and hurried into the back of the pub.

RJ stared after her as her patchwork skirt swished out of sight into the doorway.

"And we think we've got problems," she said to Stuart with a sigh.

Chapter 8

She sat at the mouth of the cave, cleaning her weapons, when the unknown man and woman stepped into view. She was confident that the darkness behind her would provide enough cover to conceal her, but she still shuffled back slowly into the gloom. The last thing she needed was to attract attention to herself. It was a testament to her skills that she had survived out here for so long, and she wasn't about to let a false sense of security undermine that. The pair didn't look like they could do her any harm, but if she was forced to kill them it would bring the others out in their droves.

She'd need to get off the estate soon, but there was still too much movement, too many threats. She'd seen and heard the patrols that searched for her day and night. These two didn't feel like a threat, but it was best to be cautious. Besides, she still had a couple of things to take care of. Nothing was going to stop her from carrying out her duty.

Nothing and no one.

From her cover of darkness, she watched as a car left the big house and made its way towards the couple. She watched as they stood talking to the driver. She watched as they got in and drove away. She watched until the vehicle was completely out of sight before she shuffled towards the light and resumed cleaning her weapons, surveying the tranquil countryside below her shelter.

Chapter 9

The car door groaned in protest as RJ pushed it open and stepped out into the hot sun beating down on the entire country.

She and Stuart had decided to divide and conquer, with her maintaining the ruse that they were looking for property while Stuart went to check out the archives of local papers in the library.

The old, rusty gray Ford she had just emerged from was not what she'd expected when the estate agent had picked her up that morning. It should have given her a clue as to its driver, who had surprised her even more. Scott Allen of Scott Allen & Son would not have instilled much confidence if she had actually been looking for property. His tweed suit, wool tie, and ruddy complexion gave the impression of a farmer rather than any form of property advisor. The car told her business wasn't exactly booming, and it made her think she'd made a mistake in arranging the appointment. There hadn't been much choice in the area, however, and her reasons for looking at property were purely spurious.

Upon entering the car, RJ smelled the sweat wafting off Mr. Allen, despite the early hour.

"I apologize in advance, Ms. Black. The car doesn't have any air-conditioning. We'll need to keep the windows rolled down."

"That's fine by me," RJ reassured him. Why on earth was he wearing such inappropriate clothing in a car with no air-con in the middle of a heatwave?

Two hours later, she was glad to escape the cloying bouquet of body odor as she stood frowning up at a large country house on a hill.

"This is way out of my price range, Scott. I can see that just by looking at it. I mean, what is it fifteen, twenty bedrooms?"

"Twenty-two. And, yes, yes. You're completely right, of course," he blustered, getting redder by the minute. "But I wanted to show you what you could get if you increased the budget. I know the owners are willing to look at offers. They've had this on the market for nearly three years, so you have an advantage with this one."

"It's massive, Scott, much too big for what we had in mind. So far, all you've shown me is a rundown barn that needs a complete overhaul, the land on the side of the hill from earlier that we can afford but can't afford to build a house on, and now this. It's all out of our budget." RJ raked a hand through her hair. This process was so exasperating, and she didn't even want to buy a property.

"All great options, in their own unique ways, for an artistic retreat, if you could just stretch your budget a little," Scott suggested, holding his thumb and forefinger an inch apart and squinting hopefully in her direction. A bead of sweat dribbled down his neck and under the collar of his shirt.

"I'll be honest, Scott. I'm not even going to go in the front door. It's not what we're looking for." She turned around to look at the view. "I do love the views, though. I think my husband and I would consider a parcel of land if we could make the construction costs work. I'd need to crunch the numbers."

"There's not much land in the area that comes up for sale," he told her reluctantly. "We were lucky to get access to the plot I showed you earlier. I understand the earthworks on that one would likely be cost-prohibitive because of the slope, but there aren't many options within your current budget."

"Seems like the Buchanan Estate pretty much takes up most of the available land." She made herself sound dejected in the hopes that she could get him talking.

"Oh, yes, that it does. They're always acquiring more land and adding to it. You might have to go further out or change your target area. The land on the fringes of the estate will never come up for sale. If you were looking ten years ago, it might be a different story, but people around here know that Buchanan will give them the best prices. They wouldn't even consider selling it to someone else. You haven't chosen the easiest area in which to find a property."

RJ pursed her lips. "Hmm, maybe. Can you take another look and see what else you can come up with? We can up the budget if needed, but not double, mind." She gave him a pointed look. "See what you can arrange for a week from today and get back to me."

On the journey back to the pub, RJ had to breathe through her mouth, face towards the window and the fresh country air. Once at the pub, she turned to shake hands with Scott Allen. Finding his palm sweaty, she dreaded to think of the state of his shirt under his heavy suit jacket. She herself was hot even though she had dressed sensibly in a short-sleeved summer dress. Breathing a sigh of relief, she entered the pub and ordered a pint of cider, and once Tracy had pulled her a refreshing pint of liquid gold, she settled at one of the tables to the side of the bar.

Socks sat on the end of the bar, systematically cleaning each paw. Each time the door opened, he stopped and looked up to see who was joining him. RJ did the same, minus the foot washing.

So far, the postman, a crisp delivery, and the resident old codger in the corner were the only other visitors. Three p.m. didn't bring much of a crowd out in the sticks, it seemed.

RJ sipped her pint and looked around the room. It looked like it hadn't changed since the place opened. Dark beams crowded the already low ceiling, the walls a dull beige, which may have at one time been white. The carpet must have been installed in the seventies, the deep-red flower pattern difficult to make out among years of grime caused by dirty feet, spilled drinks, and who knew what else. Each time the door opened, it brought in a draft that swirled round the room, emphasizing the musty smell of sweat and stale alcohol that characterized every old pub the world over. The smell of smoke was so absorbed into its very bones that even now, years after the smoking ban, the faint scent of smoke could still be noticed. RJ doubted Tracy would ever get rid of the ingrained odor, even if she ripped out the carpet and painted.

Tracy stood behind the bar, polishing glasses. She put down her cloth and looked over at RJ. "Just going to check the pumps. I'll be five minutes. Ten if I need to change a keg. If you want anything, just help yourself." She disappeared out the back, leaving RJ alone with the old geezer, who looked well on his way to becoming very merry.

Stuart was still at the library in Oban, checking the archives of local newspapers to see if he could find out anything new about the estate, its proprietor, or the deaths that had occurred there. She hadn't heard anything from him since he'd set out that morning.

It still surprised RJ how many newspapers, especially the smaller ones, didn't have their back issues online. It was an added expense these small firms just couldn't afford. It had surprised her even more that these places still had local papers—so many had found it difficult to stay afloat in this day and age. But they prevailed, which was evident in the small bundle of today's papers set out at the end of the bar. Their feline guard stood watch over the precious parcel, yet no one had been interested enough to attempt to grab one from under Socks' ready protection.

The door swung open again, bringing with it the smells of the pub. Socks lifted his head for a moment before resuming his ablutions, this time turning his attention to his fluffy tail.

RJ peered over her glass to see the gamekeeper they had met yesterday walk in and up to the bar, settling onto one of the high, well-worn, velvet-cushioned stools there. Seemingly blind to her presence, he waited, tapping the beer mat impatiently on the newly shined surface.

"She's in the back," the geezer in the corner offered.

The gamekeeper looked round to where the voice had come from and tilted his head in acknowledgement. "Cheers, Bert."

He got up from his perch and walked around to the other side of the bar. He ducked down and fumbled under the counter, coming up with a short glass, which he held up to the optics and poured a double measure. Next, he grabbed a glass from behind him and expertly began to pull his own pint. It was then that he noticed RJ watching him.

She raised her fingers and waved, coupled with a weak and conceivably believable, embarrassed smile.

He stared at her for a moment, his beer mid-flow. Regaining his composure, he managed to tap it off without spilling a drop. He turned to put his money in the till, counting out his change as if he knew the price by heart—he probably did—and walked back round to the right side of the bar.

RJ stared at his back, trying to decide whether to approach him. Before she could decide, he banged his empty pint glass down on the bar, the foam running down the insides to meet at the bottom. The whisky glass followed soon and he twisted away from RJ's view, taking quick strides back out the way he had come. The door swung on its hinges as he left.

Tracy popped her head out from the door to the stairs. "Who was that?"

"Wullie Carstairs. Put the money in the till," answered the old man, lifting his drink to point towards the cash register behind the bar.

"Oh, right." She disappeared again.

That was useful. Now RJ knew the gamekeeper's name: William Carstairs, or Wullie rather. And she also knew he drank in the pub, although that was pretty obvious, seeing as it was the only pub for miles.

RJ got up and moved to a stool at the bar, waiting for Tracy. Tracy looked worn out and she still had a whole night ahead of her, but the smile she offered RJ was friendly and warm.

"Are you comfortable enough up in your cabin?"

"Yes, it's been great, thanks. Nice place you've got here."

Tracy beamed.

"Do you always do that?" RJ asked. "Let the customers sort themselves out?"

"No choice sometimes. It's only me here for the main part. They're a pretty trustworthy lot 'round here anyway."

"The man that was just in looked a bit stressed. Lucky he could just help himself, seemed to be in a rush."

"Wullie? Oh, aye, Wullie's been coming' here since I was a wee girl, when my parents owned the place. He's got a lot on his mind lately, has Wullie," she said, picking up a rag and re-polishing the bar top that she had already rendered sparkling.

"Oh? That's a shame. He seems like such a nice man. Stuart and I met him when we were out walking the other day. He told us about the rogue stag and wanted to make sure we were safe, so he gave us a lift back."

"Aye, that stag's the least of it," said Tracy, shaking her head. "They've had no end of bother up at the estate lately."

"Bother?" RJ enquired.

"Aye, terrible business. Davie MacKay started it all, poor man. Killed himself, out in the fields. No one had an inkling. He was the last person you'd expect to do themselves in. He used to be in here a fair bit when he was younger, but I'd hardly seen him lately. He got himself a wife and a three-month-old baby, was saving up for their own house. He looked like he had it all. Then, just like that, he was gone. His wife and wee one have gone back to her mother's in Glasgow. Nothing keeping them here now. It was horrible to see what happened to that family, just horrible. That poor girl has to grow up without a dad and then find out what he did. I just can't comprehend."

She leaned back on the counter behind the bar and stared off into space. After a few minutes, she came out of her daze, carrying on the conversation as if there had been no interruption to the flow of conversation.

"An', no doubt, you'll have heard about James Sullivan?"

"I did hear something but didn't realize it had happened so close until we met . . . Wullie."

"Aye, that was on the estate as well. You would think it would slow down business, but there seem to be more foreign hunters going up there now than there ever was. Like they say, maybe there's no such thing as bad publicity. Wullie's got his work cut out for him and no chance to deal with everything that's happened. Am not surprised he's stressed."

Suddenly, Socks looked up, jumped off the bar and scampered away. Tracy's twin boys exploded through the front door, raced into the back, and clattered up the stairs to their home.

Kirsty followed a minute later, smiling at her mother and dumping her bag down before going over for a kiss.

"How was your day, love?"

"Fine, Mum. Billy Davidson brought in birthday cake and Daniel spewed everywhere. It was gross. Mrs. Mitchell had to get the jannie to clean it up. It was stinking. Can I take cake in when it's ma birthday?"

"We'll see," said Tracy, slipping Kirsty's too-big backpack back over her shoulders and pointing her in the direction of the stairs.

"That means yes!" yelled Kirsty as she walked up the stairs. "Hey, ow . . . watch it."

The boys barreled back into the pub, jam sandwiches in hand.

"Hey!" Tracy reprimanded, the look in her eyes offering no option but for the boys to go straight to her. She put a hand on each boy's shoulder, leaning in close to speak quietly to them. Her face was serious but her voice low, and RJ couldn't make out the words.

They stared solemnly at her as she spoke—her own face reflected in miniature in theirs, two times over—nodding in unison when she had finished. "Right, off you go then, and remember to wash your hands."

They ventured back upstairs at a far more leisurely pace than they had before. Five minutes later, they returned with their sister, who was grinning behind the jam sandwich wedged between her teeth. Content in the company of her brothers, Kirsty was almost bubbling over with happiness.

"Let's get the bikes," suggested one of the boys. The trio disappeared out the back door. RJ assumed they wouldn't be seen again until their mother called them in for their evening meal.

Tracy sighed. "They'll be the death of me, that lot."

"They seem like good kids. You do a great job."

"Yeah, no, they are. Still bloody exhausting, though. Believe it or not, the boys are the easiest. They have each other, and can pretty much look after themselves. It's hard for the wee one, though. She sees the bond that her brothers have while she's all on her own."

RJ's phone vibrated on the bar counter. "Sorry, I have to take this," RJ told Tracy. Reluctantly, she turned away from the wealth of information that was Tracy. A wealth of information she'd need to mine at another time.

Chapter 10

Ben's name flashed on the screen, which meant he was calling her from his home number. If he had been calling her from his office, the name on the screen would have read *Director*.

"Hey, what's up? I take it this is a social call?" She walked outside, happy to hear her uncle's voice.

"Nothing is up," he assured her. "I just wanted to check in with my favorite niece to see how she's doing."

"Your only niece," she reminded him.

"Well yes, my only, and my favorite, niece."

She could hear his smile through the phone and was instantly at ease.

"The property hunt hasn't turned anything up so far," she told him, glancing around to make sure she was out of earshot of anyone who might be in the vicinity.

Once she let herself in through the gate at the side, she took the old wooden stairs two at a time and fumbled in her pocket for the cabin key.

"All these things take time. You can't expect results so quickly," said Ben, his calm, velvety tones instantly warming her heart.

"I know. Hey, I thought we weren't supposed to get personal calls on assignment."

"You're not, unless your personal call comes from an uncle who happens to be the director of the organization and has a fully secured phone-link set up in his home."

"Fair enough." She put her shoulder to the door and shoved, pushing it firmly back in place behind her. "How are things at the organization?"

"Busy as ever. Things are very quiet at home, though. I'm thinking of getting a dog."

"A dog? You work far too long hours for a dog."

"It might be time for me to think about retiring . . ." He paused as if waiting for RJ to let the idea to sink in.

"You? Retire? Never going to happen. You'd be bored after a week and desperate to go back."

"I have hobbies. I'd keep myself busy."

"What hobbies?"

"You know I like to cook, and there would be walking the dog, of course."

"There's only so much cooking and dog walking you can do in a day. Perhaps you could write your memoirs," she said wryly.

He laughed heartily. "I'd have to shoot anyone who read it. That would keep me busy for a while, at least. Tell me, how are you getting along with Thomas?"

"I knew you told me his name before but for the life of me I couldn't remember it. That's terrible, isn't it? Only a complete cold-hearted bitch would break someone's knee and then not even care enough to remember his name. Stuart—I think I'll just stick to calling him that, it's too confusing otherwise—is fine," she informed him, keeping her voice low. The walls were thin and she had no way of knowing whether anyone was close by. "A bit of an unfortunate pairing but, you know, we'll work with it."

"Yes, I didn't realize who your partner would be until you were already on your way. I'm glad to hear it's working out. Your paths would have crossed at some point. Perhaps it's better that it happened now, so you can get it over and done with and put it behind you."

"Yeah, I'm sure we'll be fine."

"So, you're not fine at the moment, then?" Ben asked.

She should have known he'd read deeper into her tone than she'd intended him to.

"No, yeah, we are, we will be. It's fine."

"Hmmm."

She could hear the deep frown in his voice.

"Honestly, it's all good."

"What's it like being back? You okay with that?"

"I'm okay. It's not like I'm back. I'm just on assignment in a country that seems familiar. It's a surreal concept but far more normal than I thought it would be, if that makes sense?"

"As long as you're okay."

"I am. I promise."

"Okay."

"What about the case? Have you got any further information for me?"

"Not a lot, I'm afraid. We did uncover some interesting data from the financials, though. The estate appeared to break even until about ten years ago, then suddenly it started making enough to start buying up parcels of surrounding land."

"The place is huge. You have to see it on the ground."

"It seems it was always huge, but all this property acquisition has turned it into something else."

RJ looked out the window at the three siblings playing on their bikes. One of the boys was attempting to jump over a ramp made of an old paint tin and a rough plank of wood. It didn't look like it was going to end well. Poor Tracy would likely have even more on her plate to deal with before the day was over.

"Has the governor been putting on any pressure?" RJ asked him, amused at the scene outside. Every time they tried to cycle up the ramp, the wood slipped off the tin and the bikes thudded back down on the ground.

"No, he understands it's a process and just wants to get to the bottom of it. He's a patient man—plenty of experience in his position, after all. It's his sister that's proving to be a handful. Poor woman. He's trying to keep her in check, but she's not coping very well."

"I can't imagine how anyone would cope in that situation." RJ thought of the broken woman she met at the huge lake house. The mere thought of Janice Sullivan was enough motivation to ensure she got the job done. Sure, they weren't any further forward yet but there was no way RJ was going to let James Sullivan's widow down. She deserved answers. Hopefully then she would be able to grieve and move forward with her life.

"Promise me you'll be careful."

"I'll be careful."

"There'll be a lot to answer for if this death turns out to be anything other than an accident. The people involved will be highly motivated to ensure that this matter is put to rest."

"I know, I'll be careful. Try not to worry."

"Easier said than done, pumpkin."

"I know. I love you. Speak soon."

"Love you too, bye."

Just as she ended the call, one of the twins managed to get up the ramp; unfortunately, he had refined his technique and was going slow, so as not to knock the plank off again. He clearly hadn't considered what this would mean for his arrival at the top. The front wheel of the bike dropped down in front of the paint tin, the momentum of the plank coming up at the back, throwing his back wheel up and over the front. The boy flew off the bike and into the gravel, out of RJ's line of sight.

She hurried to her door. By the time she got it open, the flying boy had stood up, his right arm bloodied from elbow to wrist.

"That was brilliant! You do it," he shouted to his brother.

His twin hurried to reset the ramp. Kirsty sat on her much smaller bike, which, judging by its paintwork, was secondhand and had been spray-painted a pale green to suit its new owner. The streamers at the end of her handlebars fluttered in the breeze as she looked on in horror in the fear that she would be asked to perform the same trick.

As RJ ducked back inside the cabin, she could hear Tracy bellowing for them to, "Get inside right now."

Good call, thought RJ. How on earth did Tracy manage to do it all?

She sat on the couch and stretched her arms. Damn, she was exhausted. The prospect of another night on the floor on the couch cushions was depressing. Not that the alternative was any better, she thought as she looked over at the bed Stuart had claimed.

He chose that precise moment to return, knocking on the cabin door to let her know he was there before he entered, the bag he had slung over his shoulder looking just as empty as it had when he left that morning.

"Anything?" she asked him for form's sake, not holding out much hope.

He shook his head. "There's nothing in the local papers that the big nationals or news stations didn't cover. The stories lasted longer up here, that's all. I guess there isn't much else to report on. Probably the most exciting thing to happen in years and they couldn't find anything to top it."

"What about the other death? The guy on the estate?"

"MacKay. Yeah, there was a bit on him. Doesn't tell us anything, though. A few paragraphs on an unexpected death. The paper didn't mention suicide, but they never do. It was heavily implied, though. His obituary was printed the next day." He rubbed his eyes, so obviously tired from searching through newsprint and microfiche all day, then yawned, too exhausted to even contemplate covering his widening mouth. "How 'bout you?" he asked her, rubbing his right eye, which had started to water.

"Well, the property market around here sucks. I can tell you that."

"Do you think that'll affect our cover and our ability to stick around?"

She got up to switch the kettle on. "No, I think we're fine. I've got an estate agent searching for more properties. I've given him a week to get back to me. After that, who knows? I'm sure we'll come up with something to explain an extended stay if we have to. Tea?"

Stuart nodded gratefully and she popped a tea bag in each of the two mugs she'd set on the counter. Bending to get the milk out of the fridge, she said, "I saw our friendly, local gamekeeper today at the pub."

"Yeah?" Stuart visibly perked up at the news.

"Yeah, except he wasn't too friendly, surprisingly enough. Downed his drink, then left when he saw me. His name's William Carstairs, by the way."

"How'd you find that one out?" Stuart asked.

"One of the regulars at the pub," explained RJ, waving off the full story. "Tracy seems to know him quite well. I suppose that's only natural for a landlady in a pub in a place like this. She felt sorry for him. Says the recent deaths have been hard on him."

She handed him his tea.

"Did she have anything to say about that?" He took a sip and peered over the top his mug, waiting for her to respond.

RJ relayed everything Tracy had told her, plus the information of the estate's acquisitions.

"Why would the director phone to tell you that? It's a little below his pay grade. Is there something you're not telling me?"

"He didn't phone to tell me that, it just came up in conversation."

Stuart's raised eyebrow told her he didn't believe her.

"Oh, sorry, don't you know?" RJ said, suddenly embarrassed at their relationship and how others might view it.

"Know what?" he asked cautiously.

"We're related. Benjamin and I."

"Distantly?"

"Not exactly, no. He's my uncle."

Stuart put his tea on the coffee table and flopped down on the couch. "That's just great. The icing on the cake. I'm on assignment with the girl who shattered my knee and also happens to be favored by the big boss because he's her uncle."

"It's not like that."

He raised an eyebrow. "Is it not? How could it possibly not be?"

"I got into Kingfisher through talent and hard work. You can't even begin to imagine how hard I work and how much the trainers at HQ push me, precisely because I am Benjamin's niece. I have just as much of a right to be here as you do."

"We'll see."

"Yes, we will," RJ snapped.

Stuart got up from his seat. "I'm going to get a few hours' sleep. I suggest you do the same. We've got a long night ahead of us."

"Why, what's happening?" she asked, still seething.

"We're going back to the estate. It's a full moon tonight. We can't waste it, especially as we'll need to go in dark so as not to be seen."

A wave of disbelief slammed over RJ. "That terrain is rough. We'd be crazy to attempt something like that in the dark."

"If you've got a better idea of how we can get to the scene of James Sullivan's death, let me know. We need to investigate it somehow."

RJ folded her arms in consternation. "I don't."

Setting her tea aside, she pulled the couch cushions down on the floor and bundled herself up on her makeshift bed, too riled up to sleep.

Stuart, much to her annoyance, was soon snoring gently from the corner of the room.

Chapter 11

RJ tossed and turned in her sleep, waking groggily when Stuart shook her shoulder. He was already dressed, their backpacks at the front door, each covered in a coil of rope.

"Don't turn the lights on," he told her. "It'll make it more difficult when we leave."

RJ quickly dressed in the dark and joined him at the front door.

"We'll go over the back fence and through the trees. It would be quicker if we could follow them to the end, which is only a mile or so away from Sullivan's ridge." This was how they had come to know the cliff face where James Sullivan had supposedly perished. It didn't appear to have any other name on the maps they had found, so it was as good a name as any. "It'll be impossible in this light, though. We'll need to get out of the trees as soon as possible if we're to have any chance of seeing where we're going."

"Are we using night-vision goggles?"

"No, they're too cumbersome for the distance we need to cover. Our eyes will adjust to the low light levels. We need our peripheral vision to cover the distance we need to go. Goggles restrict your field of sight. Night vision would just slow us down and could even put us in danger because it can make you over confident. I'm trained in night observation. It'll be safer just to follow my lead."

"Right," said RJ. That was hardly reassuring. She hated having to rely on anyone else. It didn't help that Stuart was so obviously enjoying this state of power over her.

"The organization is trying to develop something more suitable, but it's not as easy as it sounds. Plus, in order to be effective and safe, you would need to put in a hell of a lot of hours in regular training. It's just not practical for the amount of time most agents in the field would actually need to use it."

Though she found his explanation perfectly reasonable, she still wished they had some form of visual help. Torches were an obvious no-no because of the attention they would attract.

They left the cabin as quietly as the stiff door allowed and climbed up the bank to the tree line. An owl hooted from above and RJ lifted her eyes to see the powerful animal swoop overhead in the direction of the village. The moon shone brightly in the sky, not a cloud in sight to obscure the little light it provided.

"Cloud cover should be rolling in around five a.m., then heavy rain for the rest of the morning. Perfect timing. Good visibility for us when we need it, and we won't need to worry about our tracks—the rain will hopefully wash away any sign that we were ever there."

They ducked under the wire fence, adjusting their packs and looking at their task ahead.

"I can't see a thing. How are we expected to get through this?"

"Your eyes will adjust. Give it time," Stuart told her. "By the time we come out of the trees into the open fields, you'll be able to see much better than you could ever imagine. You'll need to use your hands and your feet to feel the way. Listen to my voice and follow it."

RJ stretched out her hands and walked on. When she felt a tree trunk, she grasped it and swung herself around it.

"Don't look directly at whatever you want to see," Stuart said, advising her in low-light tactics and providing her with a direction in which to follow. "If you look directly at a pinpoint of light, you won't be able to see the outline of the object that the light is coming from."

"I'm hoping the only light we'll see tonight is the moon."

"Definitely don't look directly at the moon. It'll affect how well you can see when you look away. You shouldn't look directly at any bright light, and try and avoid your phone for any reason."

RJ's hand missed the next trunk and she stumbled forward, slamming her shoulder painfully into the tree. "Oof."

"You okay?"

"Yep," she muttered, grateful that he couldn't see the tears that had sprung into her eyes. She was going to have a monster of a bruise in the morning.

"Okay. Don't stare too long at any one point. Eyes tire more quickly at night if you look at something too long, so objects will disappear. And don't scan too quickly. Objects take longer to appear in your vision in the dark. Don't scan for too long, either, because that also tires your eyes."

"Got it. Don't stare too long, don't scan too long, and don't scan too quickly. I might as well just close my eyes since it doesn't seem like I'm allowed to do anything else." She rolled her eyes, knowing full well the effect was lost on Stuart. Not only was he ahead of her, he also wouldn't have been able to see her expression in the dark. She trudged on, cursing him for everything under her breath as he continued to attempt to guide her through the gloom.

RJ continued to follow his voice when, without warning, her foot caught on a root or something else unseen and she fell on her knees with a loud thud. She could add purple knees to her list of bruises to count in the shower tomorrow. They'd been walking less than fifteen minutes. How on earth were they going to make it the rest of the way? She couldn't even imagine how many bruises she'd pick up along the way.

Stuart came back and hooked his hand under her shoulder to help her up.

"I can't see a bloody thing," she protested.

"Not yet, but you will. It takes thirty to forty minutes for your eyes to adjust fully. We'll be out of the trees by then. Look, put your hand on my shoulder and I'll guide you through."

"How can you manage?"

"Training," he said grimly. "Years and years of training. Believe me, this is easier than most scenarios where I've had to practice my night vision. At least we don't need to watch out for anyone trying to blow us up or shoot us."

RJ considered the extreme situations that Stuart's time in the army, and perhaps even his time with

Kingfisher, had put him in. She kicked herself for being childish and competitive. Of course he had more skills than her in this area. She had to set aside her stupid pride and rely on his experience. She knew she still had a lot to learn, and working with and depending on a partner was the thing she had to work on the most. It was just that she hated relying on anyone else—she really needed to get over herself on that one.

She reached out and felt for his shoulder, feeling the taut muscle as she grasped it.

Stuart turned his head. "We ready?"

"Ready," confirmed RJ.

Stuart slowly walked on, with RJ following close behind him, tethered in place with flesh and bone and a renewed respect for the man she was partnered with.

With Stuart as her guide, moving through the trees was much easier. As much as she wanted to dislike the guy, she struggled to hold on to her resentment. It was hard not to forge a connection when she could feel the heat of his skin through his thin shirt, hear his breathing—emphasized by the silence that had descended upon them—so close to her own. Oh God, what was she thinking?

Abruptly, the contact broke as they stepped out of the trees and onto the vast area of pastureland. RJ was both disappointed and relieved as Stuart's shoulder pulled away from beneath her touch. Was she imagining it, or did she sense the same tangle of emotion in him? It didn't matter, she told herself. They were here to do a job. That had to be her only focus.

She turned her attention to the task at hand, amazed at how much she was able to see after the darkness of the forest. The entire area was bathed in moonlight, the hills in the distance black against the lighter dark of the night's sky. Careful not to look up at the moon in case it affected her ability to see in the dark, she chanced a look at the stars ahead of her.

Stuart watched her. "Surprising how much you can actually see, eh? Try and ignore the display above you. Direct your focus on your surroundings. That's what you need to concentrate on if we're going to get anywhere tonight." He put his hand on her shoulder, sending a current up her spine. Stuart hastily removed his hand as if he felt it himself.

RJ lowered her eyes, letting her sight readjust. "Let's go."

The walk to the ridge was much easier, with their path often dictated by what looked like deer trails through the grass. "They've already discovered the simplest way up. Makes life easier for us," Stuart explained.

"What are we looking for? What do you think we might possibly find after all this time, and in the dark?" she asked.

"I'm not sure, but we have to cover all bases. We don't know for sure that this is even where he died. Let's just wait to see what the evidence tells us. You never know what we might find—or not find. That's a bigger possibility, of course. I want to have a look at the terrain, too. See how easy it would have been for him to just fall to his death, see if it's likely or even possible."

They kept their voices low, lest their conversation drifted too far in the still, quiet, dark.

Every now and then, something fluttered overhead, making RJ uneasy. Too small to be owls, so she assumed they were bats out hunting for prey. She ducked out of reflex whenever she heard a noise in the air above her.

"What's your theory about it all?" she asked, as much as to provide a distraction to herself as to satisfy her curiosity.

"I don't have one yet. I prefer to see all the evidence."

"But you must have something in your mind."

"Nope. You obviously do, though."

"Same as I've felt all along. It wasn't an accident. I can't see what the motive could possibly be yet, but I think he was killed."

"Possibly, and actually very likely given all the evidence we have so far," Stuart conceded.

RJ's body just about purred at the warm burn in her muscles as they climbed the grassy slope. It had been a few days since she'd last trained. A run around the village roads simply didn't cut it when her body was used to a much more punishing exercise regime.

They stopped to survey the valley below them, the sheep nowhere in sight, and the atmosphere eerie in its silence. "There are no signs of life anywhere," she murmured.

"Oh, it's there all right, you just can't see it at the moment."

"I wonder if this is the way James Sullivan came up to the ridge."

"If he made it up here under his own power," Stuart muttered.

"How far is the main house on the estate from here?"

"Three miles, give or take, why?"

RJ chewed the inside of her cheek as she turned the information over in her mind. "He was out hunting at dusk. Why venture so far from the main house if he'd have to make his way back in the dark?

Odd, don't you think? And odd for him to be out on his own without a guide."

"It could be that he lost his way or maybe he just liked being on his own, especially if every second of his day was usually accounted for. Maybe this was his alone time," Stuart countered.

They marched onwards through the long grass, the sharp points slashing ineffectually at their covered shins.

"Almost there," Stuart said.

As they crested the ridge, RJ thought she could make out a dark bulge in the distance over the other side of the valley below, which may or may not have been the main house.

"The deer track doesn't go anywhere near the edge," RJ pointed out. The path through the grass followed the line of the ridge, consistently staying meters away from the black void that marked the edge. "Why would he have had any reason to get so close?"

They examined the area.

"No idea. This would be so much easier to do in the daylight."

"Maybe he saw a stag in the distance and was trying to find a shot. Or maybe he was trying to survey the area better, to see the deer or a way back to the house."

They edged closer to the brink, Stuart's arm out behind him, urging RJ to keep back. "We'll set up the ropes. I'm going to take a closer look down the cliff face." He took off his pack, knelt beside it and detached his climbing rope. When he straightened, he moved closer, peering over the side. RJ inched closer to inspect the drop with him.

"Just be caref—" the rest of his sentence was suddenly swallowed up by the sound of gravel tearing down the slope, taking him with it.

Chapter 12

RJ stood, shocked, her boots rooted in place.

Stuart had been just there, and then he wasn't.

A split second later, she dropped to the ground and cautiously crawled forward, keeping away from the area that had given way beneath Stuart's feet.

RJ didn't have time to consider that she might suffer the same fate as the tips of her fingers reached the edge, and she pulled herself closer. She peered over the edge, looking for any sign of her partner. Relief, and more than a little surprise, rushed through her as she saw the white of his face staring up at her from just over halfway down. Halfway down was still too far for comfort but much better than the alternative.

"I'm okay, I'm okay," he whispered breathlessly, but she could hear the strain in his voice.

"What's the situation?" she asked him.

"I managed to grab a bush or a tree or something on my slide down. My toes are wedged in a very narrow foothold. It's fine as long as I've got the bush to hold onto, but I don't know how long that'll last. You'll need to be quick. Please," he added, a hint of desperation creeping into his controlled response.

RJ turned her head to the darkness behind her. None of the dark shapes were big enough to be the trees that she had hoped would provide a strong anchor for the climbing rope. "It looks like only gorse. Will they hold?"

"No, the roots are too shallow. You'll need to find something else. And quick. This doesn't feel as if it'll hold out much longer."

RJ shuffled backwards, then stood up and ran to the area of darkness behind her. She frantically searched for a rock or stronger tree to secure the rope to, hands striking out, searching for options as she scanned the area in front of her. She caught sight of something in her peripheral vision to the left and changed direction to a boulder sunk into the ground. She knelt, put her shoulder to it and tried to shift it. When it didn't budge, she threw her pack to the ground and untethered the rope, winding it around and then fumbling to tie a knot Stuart had made her practice when they'd first arrived at the cabin. She closed her eyes to visualize it in her mind. It had been so much easier when she could see what she was doing. Her fingers shook as she manipulated the rope. An involuntary gasp escaped her mouth when she heard a movement in the gorse bushes. Instinct kicked in—she stopped what she was doing and looked in the direction of the noise. The darkness showed no signs of movement, gave up no further sounds. The bushes remained deathly still. RJ's heart pumped in her chest. The adrenaline must have been playing tricks on her. She shook her head to clear it. There was no time to waste on figments of her overactive imagination. She turned back to her task and tied off her knot to her satisfaction, giving it a strong tug to test its hold.

Scurrying back, she called out softly to Stuart, unable to tell where she had left him.

"Here," he answered. "Don't come too close to the edge. But hurry."

RJ got down on her belly and crawled close to where she had last looked over to see Stuart. She took the coiled rope in her right hand and swung it down towards him. It missed its mark, but it was too dark for RJ to see by how much.

"You have to get it closer," Stuart said. "I can't take my hands off this thing without having something else to grab on to."

RJ pulled the rope back up and threw it down again. This time it hit its target as it bounced off

Stuart's head. He grabbed at it with one hand, then quickly the other.

"Got it?" she called, waiting to hear his affirmative answer before shimmying backwards, then moving to ensure the rope was safely tied. RJ took it up, adding her own body weight. She couldn't fully trust that she'd managed to secure it correctly, not when there was someone else's life in her hands.

"Don't pull," Stuart's voice sounded out in the darkness. "Let me come up under my own steam."

The skin on her hands burned as she gripped the rope and listened to Stuart's agonizing grunts and moans. Twice, she heard gravel shifting and then a grunt as parts of the cliff face gave way under Stuart's feet. RJ dug her heels into the earth and leaned back against the force at the other end of the rope. She didn't realize she had been holding her breath until she felt herself gasp for air. Afraid to say anything in case it distracted him, she waited, her lungs heaving from the effort it took to hang on to the rope. The closer he got, the heavier the rope became and the more her arms ached, the muscles in her thighs burning as they locked her in place.

By the time Stuart breached the edge, he was breathing heavily and she could smell his sweat from a distance. He took a beat to gulp in some air before scrambling away from the unstable ground and collapsing on his back, his breath coming out in short, shallow gasps. RJ's body gave out and she flopped to the ground where she stood, joining him in his pursuit for oxygen.

"So, I guess we know how easy it would have been for James Sullivan to simply slip and fall to his death here." He waited to catch his breath before continuing, "I was only saved by the fact that I had been facing you when I fell. It meant I could grab at the cliff side." He paused. "If Sullivan had been looking out for deer below, he wouldn't have stood a chance if the edge gave way like that."

"Can we prove it?"

"Not without examining the area properly in the daylight, and maybe never. My slip could have covered up any evidence there might have been."

Neither was willing to move nor willing to verbalize the possibility that their investigation might have put the entire case at risk.

"Shit."

"Shit," RJ agreed. There was nothing else to be said. Reluctantly, she got to her feet. "You rest, I'll get the rope. No more investigating tonight. We need to get you back."

"Agreed," said Stuart. He was a lot of things, but foolhardy wasn't one of them.

RJ made her way back to the rock and started to untie the knot. As she unwound the rope, a bright little object on the ground caught her eye. She scanned the nearby area, trying to get a better look at it but was unable to make out any identifying features. Whatever it was, it didn't belong there. She reached out to investigate and came across what looked like a smooth, light-colored rock but felt soft and warmer than she expected. Whatever it was, it seemed out of place, so she put it in her pocket to look at later. She wound the rope into loops, reattached it to her pack and made her way back to Stuart.

She stood over him and tried to figure him out.

"All right?"

"Yeah. Thanks. I mean, thank you." He looked up at her. RJ didn't need to see the expression on his face. His tone said everything he needed to say.

"Yeah well, if you hadn't been such a good knot-tying teacher . . ."

"There is that," he admitted with a laugh.

A sudden movement in the distance caught her eye. "We've got company. Coming from the house. Look."

They watched the pinprick of light from a vehicle slowly making its way closer.

"We need to get out of here."

"Already ahead of you." RJ handed him his pack. "Let's go."

Stuart got to his feet and took a step forward, stopping as quickly as he had begun. He winced with a sharp intake of breath. "My ankle," he explained. "I must have twisted it on the way down."

RJ looked at him in dismay, glad that he couldn't see the look on her face. She hurried to him, adjusting her pack so it hung over one shoulder. Wedging her other shoulder under Stuart's armpit, she put her arm around his waist. "We'll go slow." She looked back at the car in the distance. "Well, maybe a bit quicker."

Together, they hobbled down the way they had come, stopping every few minutes for RJ to check the progress of the car, but also to give Stuart a bit of respite.

Once on the flat ground, they stumbled hurriedly along.

"There's no way I can take you back through the trees," RJ said.

"I know," Stuart said, wincing in pain. "I was thinking the same. We'll need to skirt around the road. Come out near the entrance to the estate."

"But the car—"

"We'll deal with that if, and when, we need to," he said. "Come on. We need to try to cover as much ground as possible before it catches up with us."

They floundered onwards in the darkness that had suddenly gotten thicker. She looked up to see whispery clouds start to move in over the moon. Either the forecast had been wrong, or they'd spent more time up on the ridge than planned.

As if reading her mind, Stuart said, "It's better for us, believe me. It'll be harder for them to find us. Quick, get down." He yanked her down in the tall grass and they lay deathly still, listening to the increasing rumble of the car engine coming closer. Unless the headlights passed directly over them, or the driver knew exactly where they were, they would remain unseen. They stayed down in the damp vegetation, uncomfortably close to the leftover odor of old sheep droppings. The car rumbled slowly past and they lifted their heads to see its rear lights retreat down the road.

RJ made to get up, but Stuart clutched her sleeve. "Stay down. It'll come back around."

Lying huddled together in silence with the smell of their damp sweat mingling felt unbearably intimate, and she wondered if Stuart felt the same. She was desperate to get up and get moving, to get back to safety and her own accepted personal-space requirements, but she had to trust Stuart's instinct and experience over her own desire to escape.

Sure enough, after another ten uncomfortable minutes in the grass, the headlights came back into focus. They stayed down, their white, tell-tale faces looking in the opposite direction of the car. It wasn't until the rumble of the engine was long gone that Stuart said, "Right, let's go."

Her muscles protested when she stood, and she shook her limbs to get the blood flowing again. Once again, her sympathy sparked for Stuart. The activity must have been more unbearable for him due to his injury.

She eased him up to a standing position, seeing the pain etched all over his face, and slung his cold, sweat-soaked arm over her shoulder. The immediate danger over, they took their time making their way to the entrance; as it was, they had little energy for anything other than a slow stumble towards safety.

They were both exhausted by the time they reached the gate. Their immense relief mitigated when they realized there was no way for Stuart to get through the fence without putting weight on his ankle. He let out a groan as he thrust his good leg through the space RJ had made for him, leaning painfully on his bad ankle, one arm across RJ's back as he tried to transfer as much of his weight as possible to her.

Although the road to the pub was easier going as it was flat and held no unseen surprises, it was this part of the journey that seemed to last the longest, so desperate were they to reach sanctuary. A light drizzle of rain started to fall as they neared their temporary home. By the time they reached the gate, it was pouring down, soaking them through, flowing down their faces and down their necks into their already wet collars.

"Just gets better and better," RJ muttered sarcastically as she wiped the water from her face.

"It's better," Stuart assured her, his voice tired. "The rain will hopefully erase any trace that we were even there tonight. They'll attribute the slip on the cliff to the weather, if we're lucky."

Lucky. Did she feel lucky after tonight? The events of the evening would sink in at some point, but RJ didn't know if she would call them lucky. Lucky to be alive maybe, but not lucky.

RJ eased the gate open, praying for it not to creak. The downpour helped to mask any noise it made. Once through, they broached the stairs painstakingly slowly. There wasn't room enough for both of them side by side, so RJ went ahead, walking backwards, with Stuart's hands on her shoulders and hers supporting his torso as best she could. Even then, it was slow, and she could see it was painful for Stuart. She watched him try to mask the wince on his face each time he had to bear weight on his bad ankle and found herself wincing in anticipation each time he did. The entire night had been exhausting. RJ used the last of her energy to force the door open with her shoulder. They barely made it through the door of the cabin before collapsing in a heap on the floor.

Chapter 13

She had hidden in the cover of the bushes and watched the woman who had unexpectedly turned up where she had made her kill those weeks ago. The body of the hunter had disappeared when she had returned to the scene. Now, it seemed the woman was looking for it, just as she herself had when she had first returned. The woman was remarkably close to where the body had lain, but seemed none the wiser.

She'd made a mistake in her movements and the woman had almost seen her. Luckily, the woman had been too preoccupied to investigate further. Lucky for the woman, that is. If she had discovered her, then she'd have been taken down in much the same way as the hunter had.

But the woman hadn't discovered her hiding place and another man had soon joined her. The odds were much less in her favor with two opponents, so she managed to slink away without drawing attention to herself. A shame, really; she would have enjoyed a good kill tonight.

When she turned back to look at them, the sight of headlights in the distance startled her. She broke her cover, running over and around rocks and tufts of grass, determined to outrun the people who were looking for her.

She retreated to a tight cave that had been the home of a fox before she had chased it away and settled in to watch the headlights in the distance.

Chapter 14

RJ spent the next few hours tending to Stuart's injuries. He'd cried out when she removed his boot from his bad ankle, despite how gentle she'd been. It hadn't been easy to get it off, and the boot's tightness had likely kept the swelling under control until they'd had the chance to pull the injured limb free; the footwear providing an efficient compress. The removal of his sock had revealed a mess of swollen red and purple flesh that continued to swell to a horrific size, no doubt worsened by the distance they'd had to cover to get back. She found ice in the freezer, wrapped it in a dish cloth and packed it around his ankle as best she could before elevating it on a pillow. She refilled the ice tray, knowing that she'd need to change the dressing in a few hours.

She took her first-aid kit from her pack, cursing at just how ineffective it had been out on the hills with no time or light for it to have been any use.

"Here, take these," she ordered, handing Stuart a couple of painkillers and a glass of water. He swallowed dutifully, leaning up on his arms so as not to disturb his leg. She boiled the kettle and let the water cool, adding some disinfectant to a bowl with the cooled water and plunged his scraped hands in to soak. He didn't utter a sound, but she saw the pain he attempted to hide. The fall had caused a long abrasion on his cheek that neither of them had noticed until they were back in the light of the cabin. It had taken a long time of careful dabbing with the gauze to ensure it was clean and free of debris. When Stuart's hands were as clean as they were going to get, RJ dabbed them dry with a towel, careful to avoid the areas around the tips of his nails that had been ripped off.

"I've been tortured more gently than this," Stuart told her, only half joking, before they both fell into an exhausted sleep on the bed, their animosity towards each other forgotten.

#

RJ awoke with a headache as light started to stream in the window. She got up and replaced the ice around Stuart's ankle. "The swelling's gone down a bit, but I don't think you'll be much use for the next few days." She looked up to see his reaction and was greeted by the monstrosity that was his face. As they'd slept, blood and pus had oozed out of the graze that ran the length of his cheek. The fluids had crusted over, completely engulfing his right eye. The crust formed a grotesque pirate patch that continued down towards his chin.

Her sharp intake of breath alerted him to the fact that something was wrong. "What is it? Is it my ankle? Does it look broken?"

"Your ankle is doing well," RJ assured him as she handed him some more painkillers.

"Aah . . . shit," he said as he tried to sit up and open his eyes. His hand went to his face and probed his encrusted mask. "That bad, eh?"

"It's not so . . . yeah, that bad."

"That's inconvenient, to say the least."

"Yeah, but at least you'll live to fight another day."

"Just not today," he grumbled.

"Not today." RJ tried to figure out what that meant for their investigation. She was too exhausted to devote much brain power to anything and Stuart wasn't in any fit state to add anything constructive. They'd figure out something later. Right now, what they both needed was rest.

They lay down and slept for another much-needed few hours. RJ woke before Stuart, gently eased herself off the bed so as not to disturb him, and went into the bathroom to take a hot shower. As she undressed and looked in the mirror, she realized just what a state she was in. Her face was streaked with what she hoped was mud, her hair was wild and tangled with foliage of some sort entwined in the knotted strands. Her hands were the only exposed part of her that were clean, and that was only due to her extensive cleaning of Stuart the night before. She stood under the hot stream in the shower, washing the dirt and grime off as best she could under the low pressure of the old electric shower.

She felt a lot better once she stepped out and dried off. She quickly dressed, then as quietly as she could, left the sleeping Stuart as she went to investigate the local shop for more first-aid supplies.

It didn't look like much from outside. Just a double-fronted shop under a flat. It looked to have been a large house before it was converted to serve the community. Notices and signs of special offers covered the surfaces of the windows, letting little light into the low-ceilinged and crowded interior. Halogen strip lights did the job that natural light couldn't, harshly illuminating every recess of the busy space. Being the only shop for miles, it seemed to stock everything under the sun and had an impressive range. RJ walked up and down the aisles, peering at the shelves, searching for what she needed.

"Help you there?" asked the friendly shop owner. He wore a white apron and held his thumbs in his pockets as he rolled back on his heels. All he needed to complete the look of a caricature was a well-groomed moustache.

She smiled at him. "My husband went over on his ankle when we were out walking. Stepped right in a rabbit hole." She shook her head in mock disbelief. "I'm just stocking up on anything I might need."

He held his finger up and walked one aisle over, and she trailed after him.

"Ah, then you'll need this." He handed her an elastic bandage, then rummaged about on the bottom shelf. "And maybe this. It's a gel cool pack. Reusable, and it molds to the shape of whatever body part you need it for."

She took two.

"Do you need any paracetamol or ibuprofen?"

"I'll take both." She also picked up a tube of antiseptic cream.

"And, of course, you'll need one of these." The shopkeeper lifted a bottle of Lucozade from a shelf as he led her back to the counter.

RJ looked at the panacea that every British person was well familiar with. She could almost taste the sharp orange liquid as she followed him down. It reminded her of days home from school, sick, curled up on the couch under a blanket and being tended to by either her mum or dad, depending on who could get the time off work. "Yeah, I'll take a bottle." She smiled. He was certainly good at the upsell.

"So, you're the folks looking to start up an artist colony."

Word had obviously got around about their presence in the village.

"Retreat," RJ corrected him. "And yes, that's us."

"Welcome to the area. I hope you find what you're looking for."

If there was ever anyone who knew what was going on in an area, it was shopkeepers and taxi drivers. She could use that to her advantage.

"Thanks, it's a beautiful place. We didn't realize it was affected by so much tragedy until we got here."

"Aye, the estate's had a hard time of it lately. That's for sure."

RJ waited for him to continue but he just smiled blandly at her.

"You have a nice day," he told her.

RJ left the shop more than a little bewildered. Surely if she was to get any gossip from any one, it would be the local shopkeeper?

After a quick stop at the pub, she returned to find Stuart awake and sitting up in bed.

"Supplies," she explained and lifted her bag in demonstration. "Feeling any better?"

"My ankle is." He lifted the cold compress she had draped over his foot before she'd left. It looked better than it had the night before, but it was still quite swollen and had started to turn a deeper shade of purple.

"We'll keep icing it. I've got these gel packs. We'll just keep rotating them until we're sure the swelling has gone down." She popped them in the freezer to chill. "Your face on the other hand . . ."

"That rough?" Stuart asked her. "Actually, you don't have to answer that. I can feel it every time I try to move my face."

"Here, I'll just get a mirror and you can see for yourself." She handed him some gauze along with the antiseptic cream. She unhooked the mirror on the wall in the bathroom and brought it back, sitting down on the bed beside him.

"Jesus," he said. "It's worse than I thought. This is going to be more of a problem than the ankle, isn't it?"

"Looks that way. You can't go out like that. And you certainly can't do any investigating looking like that. You'd attract too much attention. No, I think to the outside world you'll just need to be cooped up with your walking injury for the next few weeks. You did step in a pretty deep rabbit hole after all."

She let that information sink in as Stuart gingerly dabbed at the wound on his face with the antiseptic cream, his torn fingernails looking even worse this morning now that they were covered in dried blood.

"Seems like I'm a bit of a jinx for you," RJ said sheepishly.

"You've got to be kidding. You're the one who saved me. If it wasn't for you, I'd be a lot worse off this morning. Besides, I've had a lot worse than a twisted ankle and scrape on my face. You'll know all about that soon enough." His voice dropped lower. "It's a dangerous business. People get hurt."

"I know, and I'm prepared for that."

"You think you are, but the first time's the worst. Have they shot at you with Kevlar yet?"

RJ nodded. It wasn't a pleasant memory. Penelope, the organization's weapons expert, had strapped her up in a Kevlar vest then had her stand and watch while she took a shot at her. The impact had winded her and brought her to her knees. "It hurt like hell, but the psychological impact was harder."

"It's the same with real bullets, except you bleed, and depending on what they hit, it is so much more painful. It's the panic that's the worst, though." He stared over her shoulder at nothing in particular. "Never panic, that's what will put you in danger. Not the bullet wound or whatever else might have happened. It's the panic. Stay calm and your chances of recovery or even survival are much higher." He looked her straight in the eye with his good eye and gripped her forearms. "Just don't panic."

She broke the suddenly serious connection. "Whoa there. Getting a bit ahead of ourselves, aren't we? Just because you're all laid up doesn't mean I'm suddenly in more danger."

"No, I don't suppose it does." He shrugged. "Maybe I'm just reacting to being put out of action and feeling pretty useless to the mission just now." He smiled in what RJ thought might have been apology, but he actually looked like a deranged monster from a sick horror movie, his half-face mask made up of scabs distorting his expression. RJ was sure it hadn't been the look he was going for.

"Look, I'll be fine, you'll be fine, everything will be fine. I can still go about my business out there. You can do some research in here. I'll be less conspicuous on my own, anyway. A woman on her own is usually perceived as less threatening."

He laughed at that. "If only they knew."

"If only they knew," she agreed. "I'll stick around today. Which makes sense anyway for a wife to do for her injured spouse. Tomorrow, I'll go into town. I want to see the fiscal in action."

"Sounds good."

"Yeah, there's a fatal accident enquiry into a fisherman who went overboard. I want to see the sort of death he does commission an enquiry into."

"Any that don't occur on the estate, it seems."

"While I do that, perhaps you can find out just what the owner of the estate has over him. What possible reason he might have for helping them to cover up these deaths. Today, though, we rest. We both need it after last night's excitement."

"You're not going to get any argument from me."

"Good. Now for the difficult bit." She returned to the bag of groceries on the kitchen counter. "Maltesers or M&Ms," she said, holding up the bags.

"Maltesers, no question."

"And this might be contentious, but Highlander or Brave?" she asked, holding up the DVDs she had picked up from the collection at the pub on the way back.

"They didn't have any others?"

"Sure, but these were the best ones. No problem, we can watch them both." She gave him her widest grin and placed one in the DVD player. "Heaven," she exclaimed, leaning back against Stuart's good side and making herself comfy.

Chapter 15

RJ parked at the Tesco supermarket car park and made her way to Albany Street. The Sheriff Court was on the corner. It looked small from the outside—a two-story building with double-height windows on the second floor. It must cost a fortune to heat in the winter, even with the thick sandstone walls. It was less grand than she'd expected. Imposing, yes, and more austere than the municipal buildings across the road, but somehow not as dramatic as she'd thought it would look. The location up a simple road in the town center, with no fanfare or display of their power and status—other than the simple signs on the buildings—added to the anticlimactic feeling. It made sense, she supposed. The date on the building announced that it had been built in 1890, when the town was already well established. There wouldn't have been space for it in any of the more prominent positions it would have been better suited to. And they hadn't needed a bigger court due to the size of the population it served.

Still, it felt lacking in some way, and she hoped it wasn't an indication of the inadequacies she suspected of the legal establishment.

The inside was no more impressive. A sign on a brass stand told her the case she was looking for was to be held in the courtroom on the ground floor. She made her way there and found a seat in the public gallery at the back. A handful of onlookers, the victim's family and friends, and a solitary reporter at the ready with his notepad and pen were in attendance.

Procurator Fiscal Alexander Dunn sat at a table at the front, going over his notes. The gold pen in his hand hovered over the pages, coming down to scribble notes or circle certain words or passages. He was tall, even sitting down, and when he stood up, RJ was surprised at his height. He remained standing for a minute, his lips moving as he closed his eyes, his head held skywards. Sitting back down, he shuffled his notes, then leaned forward, palms together and his forefingers resting just below his nose. His jet-black hair belied his years. RJ had been told he was fifty-three, but the man in front of her looked nowhere near it. Solemn but fresh-faced, not a frown line or wrinkle in sight despite his weighty job. He didn't appear to be a man troubled by his conscience, but what that might look like she didn't know. His unfashionable Lego-man haircut indicated a disinterest in the more mundane and frivolous aspects of daily life that might have been important to others. Just what was important to Alexander Dunn?

"All rise," called a court clerk. Dunn placed his pen in line with the top of his papers, subtly adjusting its position as he stood.

The sheriff entered from a side door, his black robes flapping as he walked to his place at the front of the room. White, frizzy hair poked out from under his horse-hair wig. So many judges in the country and beyond had chosen a less formal approach, ditching their wigs and gowns in civil cases. She wondered if Sheriff McIlvanney was of the more traditional breed, or if he felt the occasion required a more somber approach. As the court sat, RJ looked across at the tear-stained face of a middle-aged woman who clutched a teenage boy in her arms as if hanging on for dear life. The boy held onto his mother and stared lifelessly at the sheriff.

RJ couldn't take her eyes off the woman and her son. It felt wrong to impose on this family tragedy, but in doing so, she might be able to provide answers to someone else going through the same pain, or maybe even prevent another family from going through the same process. If there had been two deaths already on the estate, would there be more?

The fiscal stood up to outline the case of Thom Malone, who had fallen overboard when struck by a winch on the Meriwether while fishing for cod three months previously. After a lengthy description, he called upon the captain of the boat, Kevin Haldane. Kevin held his head high and walked resolutely to the box at the front, his meaty hands held in tight fists at his sides. Throughout Fiscal Dunn's questions, this big bear of a man broke down no less than three times. He had seen his friend perish on his watch and bore the responsibility of his death as visibly as an anchor weighing around his neck.

Dunn's questioning held no place for sympathy. All the man was concerned with was the truth and getting to the details of what had led to Mr. Malone's death. He gave Kevin time to compose himself after each breakdown but displayed no emotion as he continued his inquiry. The fiscal was almost robotic in his interactions. It was difficult to tell if he cared about the people at all, but what was evident was his competence and skill. It further fueled the idea that no one would be able to pull the wool over his eyes in the case of a wrongful death.

When Kevin left the stand, it was Thom Malone's widow who moved over to comfort him in their shared grief. The sounds of their sobs mingled together in a heartbreaking harmony of sorrow.

The sheriff called a short break to allow the upset to diminish before the fiscal called upon another crew mate from the fishing boat, the marine mechanic who had installed the winch two years previously, and the doctor who had attended the scene once the boat had returned to dock with one less living soul on board.

In all his questioning, the fiscal was relentless in his search of answers. At no point was he rude or disrespectful, but his sense of authority was an overbearing power, perhaps more so than the sheriff's, who listened carefully to each witness in turn, asking questions when he felt the need for clarification.

The process lasted all day and left RJ emotionally and mentally drained. She wasn't surprised when Sheriff McIlvanney ruled it an accidental death. It seemed to her that Thom Malone had suffered an unfortunate turn of fate that no one in attendance could be blamed for. This gave little comfort to the people waiting to hear the verdict, not least of which Kevin Haldane, who would no doubt blame himself for the rest of his days. The sheriff detailed how an accident like this might be avoided in the future, so that no others had to suffer the same fate as the Malone family or the crew of the boat.

They rose again as the sheriff left. Alexander Dunn solemnly shook hands with Thom Malone's people, then left them to their tears as he strode out of the courtroom.

RJ followed, seeing him disappear down a corridor and into a room at the end.

Well, that hadn't told her anything. She was no further forward than she had been that morning. All she'd learned was that the fiscal was good at his job but was a cold-hearted brute when it came to the people he was supposedly working for. Who knows, maybe it had to be that way? RJ didn't know. She'd never had any dealings with the Scottish justice system herself. The drunk driver who had killed her parents hadn't lived to face the justice doled out by the courts.

She walked out into the fresh air of late afternoon, welcoming the breeze that eased some of the heat from the unprecedented heatwave. She stretched her arms as she walked to the corner across from the courthouse to wait. The fiscal hadn't glanced her way during the proceedings. He'd had no reason to, as his focus had been at the front of the court room. For this reason, she didn't think he would recognize her and so decided to wait for him based on a hunch. It paid off when, ten minutes after she had exited the courthouse, he came out wearing a tweed jacket and tan trousers. To him, it must have constituted as casual clothes after the formality of his court attire.

His height was more evident now that he was among other people. He towered head and shoulders above most of the men and women who passed him. A small boy clutching his mother's hand turned back to gawk open-mouthed at the giant that passed him before his mother dragged him along. He only turned his head forward once his mother reprimanded him. But the boy couldn't help a quick glance back as he got to the end of the street.

RJ followed the fiscal at a distance, wondering about this man who would never have the ability of blending into the crowd. Everyone would know who he was around here—not that anyone acknowledged him on his walk down the road. If anything, eyes were averted, roads were crossed and bodies moved aside to let him pass. Whether this was due to his physical stature or his role was difficult to tell. Whatever it was, he carried a presence about him that commanded respect. RJ was curious to know whether he was aware of his effect on people. If so, did he use it to his advantage? How?

He turned sharply at the end of the street, and RJ rounded the corner to see him duck as he entered a door ahead. She caught up and looked at the sign, which read *Stag's Head* in large block letters over a stylized print of a deer with full antlers. Making her decision in a split second, she entered the pub.

She paused to let her eyes adjust to the gloom. Spotting Fiscal Dunn sitting at table near the back, she walked to the bar and ordered a drink. Surreptitiously checking out her surroundings as she waited, she concluded that the tables at the front would be the least conspicuous for her surveillance. She handed the barman a five-pound note and told him to keep the change before retreating to a table near a window. The window barely provided any light due to the grubby brown curtain that was pulled across the patterned glass. She lifted the newspaper that had been left on the table beside her, opened it, and tried to look absorbed in the articles within.

She glanced up when she saw movement near the fiscal's table. A barman set a glass and a half-full bottle of Laphroaig whisky on the table in front of him, returning to add a jug of water. Alexander Dunn smiled for the first time that day as he thanked the barman and poured himself a generous measure, tipping in a modicum of water from the jug. He took a swig, grimacing slightly as the amber liquid hit the mark. He swirled the glass and took another sip before sitting back to watch the front door.

As if on cue, the door opened and Wullie Carstairs walked in, heading straight for the fiscal's table. The fiscal stood and shook Wullie's hand before he signaled for the barman to bring another glass.

RJ took a pen from her pocket and pretended to do the crossword.

The men were loud, but she couldn't make out what they were saying. At one point, Fiscal Dunn threw back his head and laughed, Wullie's shoulders shaking at the shared joke. Whatever their business was together, it seemed to be personal. The fiscal attempted to top up Wullie's glass, but the gamekeeper waved him off with a shake of his hand. Wullie filled up his glass with water and slowly sipped on it. Alexander Dunn didn't seem perturbed as he topped his drink off with another shot of whisky. The men chatted amiably, and eventually, they stood up, shaking hands. This time, the fiscal put his hand on Wullie's upper arm in an unexpected show of warmth.

Wullie sauntered out of the pub, oblivious to RJ's presence. Alexander Dunn helped himself to another double measure from the bottle in front of him.

RJ couldn't figure out their connection. It had to have something to do with the estate.

The barman went over to the fiscal's table, then returned ten minutes later with a plate of fish and chips, which Alexander Dunn got heartily stuck into.

On seeing this, her own stomach grumbled in envy. Seeing no point in tarrying any longer, RJ stood up and left the pub.

Chapter 16

When RJ entered the cabin, Stuart was still on the bed. "Been there all day?"

"Just about," he replied. "But I've probably had a more productive day than you."

"Probably." She told him about her impressions of the procurator fiscal in court and his meeting with Wullie Carstairs.

"Well, that I can't explain," he said, puzzled. "I did a little digging into the lack of fatal accident enquiries for Sullivan and the suspected suicide on the estate."

RJ's eyebrows arched upwards in question.

"I phoned the procurator fiscal's office and asked them about it."

"You just phoned them up and asked," she said incredulously. "If we had known it would be that simple, we could have done that days ago."

"'Simple' is stretching it a bit. I had to do a bit of minor phone hacking to disguise my number, then reroute their phone calls to a helping hand at Kingfisher, who bounced it back to me."

"Who did you say you were?"

"Monopolies Commission, investigating the land grab from the Buchanan Estate and questioning why the deaths that occurred there hadn't had fatal accident enquiries."

RJ doubled over, laughing until tears leaked out of her eyes. "Monopolies Commission . . . oh my god." The stress she'd held onto since the night of Stuart's fall eased with her uncontrollable laughter. She didn't understand why she found it so funny, but she couldn't stop laughing. Normally, something like that would have simply been amusing, but for some reason, at that precise moment, it was the funniest thing she'd ever heard.

Every time she looked up at him, she fell back into hysterics. If there was ever a man who didn't look like he was calling from the Monopolies Commission, it was the man in front of her, huddled on an old bed in a tiny cabin at the back of a pub, one leg elevated and still iced, his face making him look more like the Phantom of the Opera than a government official.

"Classic. I still can't see how you pulled it off, but that's a good one." She finally regained control of herself, wiping her eyes dry with a tissue. "What did you find out?"

With a shake of his head and what she assumed was supposed to be a derisive glare, Stuart continued, "His paralegal wouldn't tell me anything, of course, especially not right away, so I had her look into the website and phone back on the official number. Which she did, except one of our friends at HQ intercepted the call, acted as the operator, and then transferred her to me. Very nice lady she was, too. Naturally, she couldn't talk about specifics for the case, but she did tell me some interesting general information."

"Such as . . ."

"For the shooting, the doctor on scene pronounced it as suicide. The estate called the police. They actually called them in first. The police called for the doctor. The investigation had already been done. In fact, it sounds as if the death wasn't even reported to the fiscal since it was ruled as a suicide. It wasn't a work-related accident. It just happened at work, so there was no need for an official inquiry. Seems to be a gray area, but sometimes it just happens, apparently."

"Doesn't seem right to me."

"No, but I don't think it points suspicion onto the fiscal."

"But what about James Sullivan? Surely it's odd that there was no inquiry into his death?"

"Well, according to the paralegal, an inquiry usually starts when a coroner takes control of the deceased in their home country. A mix-up at the funeral home when a body is mistakenly cremated isn't something they've come across before. There's no precedent for what to do in that case. Fiscal Alexander Dunn got a report from the police and the doctor, who the police called. Supposedly, he passed this on to the relevant authorities in Sullivan's home state."

"She told you all of this?"

"I read between the lines."

"What does this mean for us?"

"Well, it means the fiscal didn't cover anything up."

"Do you honestly believe that? What about his meeting with Wullie Carstairs? Plus, I saw him in action. He got right down to the bare bones of the truth in the fatal-accident hearing today. He gives the impression of the kind of person who does everything by the book, doesn't stop until he gets to the truth. The man's a machine, Stuart. Stuff like that just wouldn't slip through the cracks."

If Stuart's face could move enough to show any emotion, he would have looked mightily confused. As it was, he only looked monstrous. He sighed. "Aarrgghhh. Now I don't know what to think."

"I do. If I hadn't seen him in action and hadn't seen him meeting the gamekeeper, then I'd be inclined to go along with your theory. But I did see him. What you found out doesn't put him in the clear. What it does tell us, however, is that there are more people involved. The local police and the doctors are involved for a start. Not to mention the funeral home."

Stuart sighed. "It can't be so big. We can't cast our net that wide, can we?"

"Is there any way for us to find out which police officers were on the scene? I agree with you, the whole lot of them can't be in on it."

"I'll put in a request." He looked up at the ceiling. "The doctors' names are on the death certificates. I'll try and book an appointment with one of them. I do look like I need some medical intervention, after all."

"Might as well try and use it your advantage."

"Speaking of using things to our advantage, there are some times when it might be less suspicious if you investigate things on your own, instead of going as a couple. Your husband has arranged a day out for you to make up for the fact he's stuck here, unable to go out."

"What have you done?" RJ asked, suddenly suspicious. She narrowed her eyes, waiting for him to explain.

"Nothing terrible, I promise. I booked you in for clay pigeon shooting at the estate, followed by a grouse dinner with the other shooters."

RJ released the breath she'd been holding. It wasn't as bad as she had suspected. "What on earth am I supposed to wear to that?" she pondered out loud.

"Don't worry about that. I've ordered you an outfit, appropriate for the occasion. It should arrive by special delivery tomorrow."

She picked up one of the scatter cushions on the couch and threw it at him. "Now you've got me really worried."

Chapter 17

RJ phoned the local doctor's surgery early the next morning. The receptionist greeted her with a cheery, "Hello, Maxwell Medical Practice, how can I help you today?"

"Hi, I'd like to arrange a house call for my husband. We're here on holiday and he's unfortunately had a fall. His face is pretty bad and I'm not sure if his ankle is broken or just sprained."

"You really should take him to A&E, dear, up at the hospital. They'll be much better equipped to deal with any broken bones."

"Oh, but it happened a few days ago, and the thing is, now I've gotten him up all these stairs, I don't think I'd be able to get him back down," RJ explained. "We're staying in one of the cabins at the pub in Ferlieclachan, you see. If the doctor could come out and check on him, then at least we'd know if we'd have to figure a way of getting him out, or if he just needs to rest. I'm quite concerned about the graze on his face. I'm worried it's infected. We're just at a loss of what to do and would really appreciate the doctor's advice." RJ hoped she'd managed to play her role of concerned wife well enough to play on the woman's sympathy.

"Let me just check to see what I can do. The doctor does his house calls until eleven every day and you've called quite early, so . . ."

RJ heard computer keys clicking in the background.

"Dr. Maxwell can come out at ten-thirty this morning. Shall I book you in?"

"Yes, that would be fantastic. Thank you," RJ said before giving her Stuart's details.

RJ looked at Stuart. "That was too easy. When have you ever had a suspect make life so much easier for you by doing a house call?"

"There's a first time for everything. Maybe this fall was good for something after all."

RJ arched her eyebrow in his direction.

"I'm not saying it was a good thing, just well, let's use it to our advantage is all."

RJ tidied away the breakfast dishes and started to tidy the cabin. What was it about doctors that made you want to appear at your best, even this one who was a person of interest in a potential murder case?

#

There was a knock on the door at ten-thirty sharp. RJ opened it to find a small gray man who looked as if he needed to see a doctor of his own. His ashen skin looked about ready to melt right off his face. The effect was worsened by the gray suit that hung on his frame and his uncombed gray hair. Here was a man who had long since stopped looking after himself.

"Dr. Maxwell to see Stuart Black." He peered over her shoulder to see Stuart in the bed within.

"Come on in," said RJ, making way for him to enter.

"Yes, I can see you've been in the wars," the doctor said to Stuart as he looked for a place to set his bag.

RJ pulled one of the dining chairs over to the side of the bed. The doctor set his bag down, opening it up in one swift move.

He snapped on a pair of latex gloves. "Let's look at that face first, shall we?" He turned Stuart's face to the light and muttered a few ambiguous "ums" and "ahs", gently prodding at the crust. "I think your own body has done the job of looking after you on this one. All this here is caused by your body getting rid of any dirt or foreign bodies that were left in your abrasions. If you let it all dry out, you'll be fine. It's likely you'll end up with minimal scarring. It looks worse than it is really."

"Good to hear. Thanks, Doctor. We've heard good things about your practice and your good self. I really appreciate you coming out to see me."

"Not a problem." He chuckled, and the sound made RJ's skin crawl. His laugh seemed hollow in his body, haunting.

"You didn't exactly have much choice, there's only me that covers this village and the surrounding area. You wouldn't have gotten any Oban doctors to come out this far."

"Oh?" RJ said innocently. "I heard there was another doctor at your practice, too."

"Nope, just myself and a nurse . . . you might be thinking of a locum we had recently."

"I must be. I think someone mentioned your locum to me. He must have made quite an impression on her. Do you tend to stick to the same ones?"

"Oh no, we can never get the same one twice, you know."

"It's someone different every time?"

"Every time. There's a bank of them, you see, and it's always changing. Usually just the new doctors, trying their hand out to see if they want to work in a rural setting. It's not for everyone. Country medicine's quite different from city medicine. You've got to be a bit of a one-man band out here—no one else to rely on, you see. In towns, if someone gets stabbed or has an accident, they get taken to a hospital. Here, if there's an accident with farm machinery or the like, then the local doctor is first port of call. It's not the sleepy job that most expect it to be."

He laid his hands gently on Stuart's ankle and prodded carefully.

Stuart grimaced slightly, but it seemed to be more for effect than actual pain.

"Have you been bearing weight on it?" the doctor asked as he continued to examine the area. The purple bruising was fading to green.

"Only on trips to the bathroom," Stuart admitted. "It wasn't pleasant at the time, when I went over on it, I mean. I had to use it more than was probably wise in order for us to get back to the car after the fall."

"No, not ideal. And how does that feel? When you do bear weight on it?"

"Better than yesterday, which in turn was better than the day before."

"Hmm . . . I'd hazard the opinion that it's not broken. You're very lucky, actually. The bruising is healing nicely. The pain at the start was most likely due to inflammation, worsened by the fact that you had to walk on it afterwards. I'd continue to rest it and just listen to your own body. If anything feels painful, stop. Also, when you do start using it again, take it slowly. It might not hurt at the time, but you might suffer for it afterwards. Be careful to build up your exercise. Don't rush things." He smiled, but it seemed like a poor act. He was certainly saying the right things, but his attention seemed to be somewhere else. His body may have been in the room with them, but his mind and soul were oddly absent.

Stuart nodded, listening intently.

"I'll give you something for pain relief to see you through." He scrawled on a prescription pad. "I'm also going to put a compression bandage on there." He handed the prescription to RJ. "You'll be doing the honors, no doubt?"

"Thank you."

"Yes, thank you, Doctor. You've been very helpful. We appreciate you coming out."

"Not a problem. I hope you're back on your feet in no time." He searched through his bag for a compression bandage, then wrapped it quickly and expertly around Stuart's foot and ankle, securing it in place with a pin. He smiled his hollow smile at Stuart once he'd finished. With that, he gathered his paraphernalia and exited the cabin, his mind clearly already on his next patient.

RJ closed the door behind him and moved over to the window to watch him make his way down the stairs and out the gate. His walk was brisk but there seemed to be an underlying lethargy in his movements. She couldn't quite pinpoint what she felt more than that, except that he seemed conservative in his energy. Maybe that wasn't quite right, either.

She turned back to the bed. "What did you make of him?"

"Seemed pretty competent. If nothing else, I'm glad to get a good prognosis on my injuries."

"There's something off about him, though, something under the surface that isn't right."

"I agree. Alcoholism would explain some of the signs and is surely the most obvious conclusion to draw, but he isn't an alcoholic—we'd have been able to tell. I do think your hunch is right, though. Something's going on with him. Text in, ask them to check the doctor's medical history, call history, and internet usage."

"Internet usage?"

"Just a hunch."

RJ took out her phone and did what he suggested.

"What about the whole locum thing? What did you think about that?" She tapped her fingers on her opposite hand, working through her own thought processes. She was asking herself the question just as much as she was asking him.

"I think it's much easier to pull the wool over the eyes of a young locum, someone less experienced and not used to rural life. Hell, we don't know, it may have been his first gunshot death."

"Maxwell, on the other hand, he'd have seen his fair share of just about everything out here. There's no way anyone would have been able to make anything else look like a fall. He might be weird, but he's been around the block a few times. He knows what's what."

"No, unless he was pushed. Then the good doctor would be none the wiser."

RJ sighed. "So, it is highly possible, or even likely, that the fiscal had nothing to do with the deaths and the doctors may be uninvolved, too. What does that leave us with?"

"Everything leads us back to the same thing."

"And what's that?" RJ asked.

"The estate. The answer's got to be on the estate."

"Yeah, well, Muggins here will hopefully be able to unearth something else when she goes shooting on the estate." She pulled on her shoes and left him to think while she went out to fill the prescription. It gave her a chance to think things over as she drove, but when she returned from the pharmacy on the outskirts of Oban, she still hadn't come up with any theories.

Three hours after RJ had texted in her request, her phone beeped. She raised her eyebrows at Stuart and was met with the same gesture.

"Nothing suspicious in his phone records," RJ told him, scanning the message on her phone. "They also checked his bank accounts, nothing there either. Nothing medical. His wife got diagnosed with cancer three years ago."

"I wonder if he needed cash for private treatment."

"Doesn't seem like it. She died eleven months ago."

"That could explain why he looked like death himself. What about the internet?"

"Nothing suspicious."

"I would have put my money on internet gambling."

"It doesn't seem like he has the time for any of that. Poor man." RJ suddenly felt bad for suspecting him of helping to cover up a murder.

"It doesn't let him off the hook, you know," Stuart said.

"I know, but it seems a lot less likely that he's involved."

Her phone beeped again.

"What now?" Stuart asked, his head lifted as if he could see over the top of her phone from across the room, impatient to hear what was going on. Working with a partner was always a challenge for agents who often preferred to work alone. This whole business of filtering information through someone else was wearing thin. She could imagine that it was even more frustrating for Stuart as he was now confined to the small, square footage of the cabin, unable to actively investigate the case, relying on a much less experienced agent such as RJ to do the running about and heavy lifting—as it were.

RJ held up a finger to silence him as she read the message. "The locum's moved on to a number of different practices. All his financials check out. Nothing out of the ordinary."

"Probably as we suspected then. Buchanan, or someone working for him, covered up the killing of one of his employees, or it really was a suicide."

"Coincidence?"

"I read a quote someplace that said 'Coincidence is the word we use when we can't see the levers and pulleys.' I think the writers' name was Bull, if I'm remembering correctly. I usually do."

"In this case, I feel like Ms. or Mr. Bull, whoever they may be, might be right."

"I think so. The more we find out about this case, the less we know. But what we do know leads us back to something dodgy going on at the estate. We need to come up with a game plan for your little visit."

Chapter 18

It wasn't until the next morning that RJ remembered the object she'd found the night of Stuart's accident.

Stuart stared at it as he held it up in front of his eyes. "It looks like bone to me. Skull bone most likely, a piece of it anyway."

RJ took it back. "That's what I thought when I saw it back here in the light. Up on the hill, I didn't know what it was. I just knew that it didn't belong there."

"It doesn't tell us anything, though," Stuart said. "You saw the amount of sheep up there, there's rabbits, foxes, probably stoats, others. The likelihood of it being human is small."

She frowned at the fragment that looked so fragile. It was difficult to imagine that it had once protected anything as vital or delicate as a human brain or an animal brain.

"It's just . . . I don't know, it's so close to where Sullivan died—"

"But at the top of the hill, instead of the bottom."

"Exactly. So, if it does belong to James Sullivan, his death didn't occur the way it's been reported."

Stuart frowned. "Just playing devil's advocate for a minute, but what about scavengers? He wasn't found for an undisclosed amount of time and even when they bagged him up and took him out, they might have missed a piece. It could be argued that there was plenty of opportunity for some animal to come along and forage for food."

"No." RJ shook her head as she studied the bone fragment. "If we find out it is human, the scavenger theory doesn't sit right with me. If it was found nearby or further down the hill, then fine, but that's a steep climb straight back up the cliff or at the very least a long, circuitous route back to the top. If this is James Sullivan's bone, then I'm betting he was killed at the top, or at least his body was at the top before he somehow ended up at the bottom of the cliff. There's also the possibility that if it is human, we could have another suspicious death on our hands. There could be something in that area that leads to people being killed."

Stuart propped his chin on his hand. "I'm inclined to agree. If it is human, then it has implications for our investigation, whether it belongs to Sullivan or not. But, and it's a very big but, the chances of it being human are low. We need to get it tested."

"How are we supposed to do that out here?"

"I've been with the organization a lot longer than you, sometimes they still surprise me with what they have available and where. I'd say, though, the most likely solution would be to courier it somewhere."

"We can't just hand it over to a courier!" The thought was preposterous. "It could be a vital piece of evidence."

"It'll be safer and much faster than any other option, believe me. I can't take it anywhere in this state, and we need you here, especially since I'm out of action. Look, I'll phone it in while you go and get what we need—padded envelope, tape, gauze or something to wrap it in. We'll need that whatever we end up doing with it."

RJ tasted blood from her inner cheek, which hurt from the chewing she had been doing on it since the night before. "It doesn't seem right." None of it did. Perhaps when she'd been on the job longer, she would learn to detach herself from it. She'd have to, if she wanted to stay with the organization.

#

When she got back, Stuart handed her his phone with the address of the medical research facility she was to send the suspected bone fragment to. "They're sending a bike courier up from Glasgow. He'll be up in two hours. It'll draw less attention to us if you meet him in Oban."

RJ nodded in reluctant agreement as she carefully wrapped what could be the last piece of James Sullivan in existence in gauze, before wrapping it in cling film and inserting it into the envelope. If it was him, she hoped it would make its way home eventually. The family deserved to have him with them.

#

As she drove past the sign for the funeral home where James Sullivan's body had been prematurely cremated, RJ felt the itch to go in. Dow and Sons seemed to be prospering. The building was freshly painted and a variety of shiny, gray hearses sat outside. In a town that relied on the summer tourist season to see it through until the next spring, it seemed the only year-round certainty was death.

She had no conceivable cover for entering the premises and no way of finding what she needed to know without generating suspicion. Even so, the bone fragment on the seat beside her threatened to burn a hole through its package and the car seat it sat on. It took all of her willpower not to turn the wheel into the car park.

She hesitated as she handed the courier the envelope. "You'll go straight there? You don't have any other pickups on the way?"

"No, Miss. This is the only thing I am concerned about this morning. It'll get there, don't you worry."

RJ's hand stayed clasped around the parcel as he tried to take it. Reluctantly, she let it go. The courier put it in his pack, which he swung over his shoulder, before revving his engine and disappearing down the road that led back to the central belt. RJ watched him until he was out of sight, feeling like she was missing something.

As she drove past the funeral home again, she stopped on the side of the road and made a U-turn. Goddamn it, she'd think of something to say when she went in.

A woman, who looked to be the same age as her, was showing an old man and his daughter out as RJ walked through the door.

"If there is anything at all that we can do to help, please don't hesitate to call us," the woman told the man as she clasped his hand in hers.

He nodded his thanks and allowed himself to be led outside.

The funeral director's attention immediately turned to RJ and she smiled gently in welcome. "How may we be of service to you today?"

"I'm looking for Mr. Dow."

The funeral director's manner immediately changed. The expression on her face turned from welcoming to decidedly not. "He's not available at the minute. Can I ask why you are enquiring after him?"

"My dad was a friend of his," RJ said, improvising. "Is he about? My dad would never forgive me if I came all the way to Oban and didn't look him up."

"Oh," the woman replied, still on guard. "And how do our fathers know each other?"

"They were pen-pals when they were boys. He must have mentioned him?" RJ took a punt on a practice she assumed many school children would have partook in back when Mr. Dow was a boy. She was unable to think of any other conceivable scenario why a funeral director in Oban might know someone from the south from way back.

The funeral director visibly relaxed and RJ heaved an invisible sigh of relief.

"He did mention something before, when our class at school got pen-friends from a school in France. I hadn't realized he had such a strong connection. Sorry, I thought that you were . . . it's all right, it doesn't matter."

"You thought I was what?"

The internal struggle was evident before she answered. "A journalist or lawyer or something. You're not, are you?"

"Me? Most definitely not." RJ chuckled at the absurdity of the idea then feigned concern. "You're not in trouble, are you?"

"No. It's nothing. It's fine. It's been a hard few months, that's all. Dad retired unexpectedly, and I've had to step in to take over. It's all been a bit much." She shook her head. "Sorry to lay that on you when all you've done is come in to say hello to your father's old friend."

"Not at all, don't worry about it." RJ put her hand on the woman's arm and guided her over to a chaise where thousands of people had likely been comforted before. "What about your brothers? Where are they?" RJ asked as she looked around.

"Brothers? Oh, you mean the sign. Folks round here are just too traditional to see 'Dow and Daughter' out front. They can handle the thought of me running the place fine, but to see it in black and white, well . . . This place hasn't quite caught up with the rest of the world yet. It's just me and a couple of employees. Everything's such a mess. Not exactly how I envisioned taking over the family business."

"What happened? You don't need to tell me if you don't want to. I hope your dad's okay?"

She sniffed. "Actually, you're the first person in months who doesn't know our personal business, and the first person who's actually given enough of a crap to ask." She put her hands on her knees, lowering her chin to her chest. "We didn't realize anything was wrong with Dad until he started making some mistakes around here. Some pretty big mistakes. We think he managed to hide or explain away his symptoms for a while. I don't think he wanted to consider the possibility that he was losing his mind . . . that's what he calls it anyway. The doctors call it the early stages of dementia. I'll tell him you dropped by. There are no guarantees he'll remember your father, but it might cheer him up. He tends to remember a lot more from his past, but he has his good days and bad days."

A ringing pealed out from a nearby office. "Duty calls," she said, standing up and walking hurriedly to answer the call. "Dow and Sons, how may we be of service?" Her voice was friendly, yet sincere, her own upset brushed aside to better serve whomever needed her on the other end of the phone.

The whole dementia thing could be a clever and convenient ruse, but RJ didn't think so. She stood up and took one last look before leaving as quietly as she'd come in. She didn't hear the funeral director follow her out, didn't hear her voice as she closed the car door and drove off.

"Wait, you didn't tell me your father's name!" A nonchalant shrug was all that the funeral director could afford before getting back to her melancholy workload.

#

RJ was subdued when she returned from the hand over, and glad that all they'd planned to do that day was research the estate online. The website didn't tell them anything that they didn't already know. Clay-pigeon shooting lunches were available twice a week, once during the week and once over the weekend. Sometimes Buchanan himself was around on these days, but it wasn't a given. Other hunting packages (accommodation provided) were available on request, and so exclusive as to not even make the website. RJ wondered about the clientele of a place like the Buchanan Estate. You just knew if there were no prices, then the cost would be prohibitive except to those for whom money was no issue. People like James Sullivan, for instance.

A knock on the door in the late afternoon had RJ opening the door to find little Kristy holding a package out to her. "This is yours," she said before bouncing off back down the stairs, no doubt eager to try and get involved in whatever her brothers were up to.

RJ took the package inside and set it on the bed. "I dread to think." She shook her head at the thought of the hunting clothes that lay therein.

"Don't worry," Stuart told her. "I didn't choose it. I just told the powers that be what you needed it for."

"That's reassuring, but only slightly." She rolled her eyes at the thought of what hideous attire awaited her.

"Here goes nothing," she said, taking her knife from her ankle strap and slicing the end of the package open. She put her hand in and pulled out the contents, spilling them onto the bed, and was pleasantly surprised by what she found. A sage-green, long-sleeved shirt, easy to move in but not too baggy so as to interfere with the gun; a stylish shooting vest padded at the shoulder to minimize recoil; expensive-looking, long gray pants; and a pair of slender walking shoes that would no doubt be completely useless on a hike but were perfect on a country outing for the rich, upper class. It all seemed perfectly suited, but she did worry whether she might be too hot in the unusually hot summer.

Stuart seemed to know what she was thinking in that uncanny way he had. "If you give me the top and run down to the shop for a needle and some thread, I can shorten the sleeves for you."

RJ gave him a dubious, disbelieving look.

"Honestly, it'll look as good as new. My dad was a designer for one of the big fashion houses. I was brought up sewing and messing around with fabrics."

"Huh. Not what I would have expected you to say," said RJ, looking at the rugged, and currently messed up, man on the bed in front of her.

"You'd be surprised how often that skill has come in handy over the years I've worked for the organization."

RJ raised her eyebrows but Stuart chose not to elaborate, so she did as she asked and went off to find a sewing kit. She figured she must be turning into the local shop's best customer and wasn't in the slightest surprised when she found just what she was looking for on a shelf near the back. The village did have a make-do-and-mend vibe after all.

RJ returned with the needle and thread in a few minutes and Stuart got to work.

"It makes me feel useful at least," he said as he cut the majority of the fabric from the sleeve and started sewing.

RJ left him to it as she picked up her beeping phone. *Connection found between Alexander Dunn and William Carstairs.* An old, black-and-white photograph followed, showing a class of smartly dressed boys and girls. The children in the photograph didn't look much older than Kirsty. RJ scanned the faces of the boys, zooming in close on each one. She couldn't see a resemblance in any of the boys to either Dunn or Wullie Carstairs. She showed the picture to Stuart. He peered at the faces, then shook his head, as oblivious as she had been.

Any further info to help identify? she asked via text.

A list of names came through, followed by another picture. RJ looked at the list, located the right names, and returned to the school photo. Both men stood beside each other as boys. Unlike the others, they were smiling, or at least trying not to smile as they shared some kind of private joke. They looked, to all intents and purposes, as thick as thieves.

She opened the next photo to find Wullie Carstairs' wedding certificate. It was publicly available online, but there had been no reason for anyone to go looking for it before now. It had certainly never occurred to her to search for it. She read through the document, drawing a sharp breath when she got to the witnesses. There, in black and white, was the name and signature of a Mr. Alexander Dunn, Student of Law.

"They know each other," RJ told him. "They've always known each other. The fiscal must have been Wullie's best man at his wedding. This just keeps getting weirder and weirder."

"But what does it mean?" Stuart asked as he took the phone from RJ and scrutinized the document.

"It could mean anything." RJ flopped down on the bed. "But what it does mean is that we aren't closer to any answers. They could just be old friends, and it could have nothing to do with Sullivan's death, or . . . or they could be working together. Something tells me it's the latter." She lay back on the bed, legs swung over the side, and stared at the ceiling as if the polystyrene tiles could give her some insight into what was going on.

"Saving an old friend's skin could be reason enough for helping to cover up a couple of deaths. But do you really think so?" Stuart asked.

"They're up to no good, I can feel it."

"See what you can find out on your hunt tomorrow," he said, throwing the finished garment her way.

She stood up and peeled off her t-shirt to try it on, pulling the gun vest over it. “Perfect,” she said, surprised at the neatness of his stitches. If she hadn’t watched him do it, she’d never have noticed the sleeves hadn’t been stitched with a machine. His ability to complete both arms in the short time was amazing. “How do I look?”

“Like you belong at a hunt. That Buchanan lot had better watch out.”

Chapter 19

A man was waiting for her at the entrance gates when she drove up. He wore the obligatory uniform of wax jacket and boots, but as she neared, she realized his face belonged to a much younger man than Wullie Carstairs.

"Morning, Miss," he greeted her, tipping his hat in a move that immediately made her feel like she'd stepped back in time. "Here for the shoot? Just follow the road for about three miles. When you get to the house, they'll show you where to park." He pulled the gate open for her and stood aside to let her pass.

RJ thanked him and drove on. It felt strange to be welcomed onto an estate from which she had been unceremoniously escorted from only days before, an estate that had almost caused the death of her partner. If anyone had discovered evidence of their visit, she had yet to hear about it.

The now-familiar road wound through hillocks and around corners, following the shape of the land. It ended at a grand, blonde-sandstone building complete with a working fountain, resplendent with marble deer frolicking in the water. The fountain was set between a pair of staircases that led to a long terrace in front of the house. The fountain and staircase reminded her of the Sullivans' summer home. She had thought the Sullivan house was imposing, but this was something else. The sandstone blocks of the courthouse in town had looked harsh and severe—simple-cut blocks put together in practical form. Here, the same stone had been used in a romantic and decorative way in the pillars, the window surrounds, and even in the gargoyles—the likes of which RJ had only seen on religious buildings. The gargoyles seemed to have been replaced recently, their fine features likely worn away as a result of the sandstone's tendency to weather. The upshot of the fine, decorative nature of the house was that it was far more imposing and grandiose than any of the buildings in town. This was where the real power in the area was housed.

The gravel crunched beneath her tires as another estate employee, dressed in the requisite uniform, directed her to a parking area to the right of the building. She pulled up in line with the cars already parked there. Stuart's humble Saab stood out like a sore thumb alongside the

Land Rover, Porsche, and Tesla that looked fresh out of the showroom.

She smoothed down her braid and put on her flat cap, looking in the rearview mirror as she adjusted the cap. When she stepped out of the car, the employee's friendly face greeted her.

"Please follow me, Miss Black. I hope you found us okay?"

"I did, thank you. I'm staying in the area."

"Excellent. We're just waiting for one more couple before we get started," he said as he led her to a group of men waiting on the front lawn.

"Gentlemen, this is Miss Riley Black."

A wide man with a bulbous red nose held out his hand. "Marshall McDade, pleased to meet you." RJ immediately pegged him as the owner of the Land rover.

"Terrance Stock," said the next man, offering his hand. Tesla, RJ decided, noticing his lean physique and healthy glow that suggested a plant-based diet.

"Bertie Wainstock," offered the next man, clasping her hand with a sweaty palm. His outfit looked as new as RJ's. She wondered if it was his first time.

"A pleasure to meet all of you."

A radio sprang into life, interrupting any further talk between the guests. "Main office to John one."

The employee, now identified as John, took the radio from his belt and walked out of range of the visitors. After a few minutes, he returned and informed them that there had been a cancelation and no one else would be joining them.

"Let's get started, shall we?" he said with a cheery smile. "Mr. McDade, Terrance, please bear with me as I run through the safety briefing, I know you're both dab hands at this."

He rattled through the briefing on autopilot before handing out ear protectors and unlocking a case on the back of his truck to hand them each a gun. "These are Winchester Selects Mark 2, familiarize yourself with it. We'll be shooting in pairs—the trap will release two clays in quick succession. The shooter here"—he pointed to the left-hand mark on the ground—"will aim for the first target, and the shooter here"—he pointed to the right—"will aim for the second target. Any questions?"

The men in the little group shook their heads.

"I do," RJ announced sheepishly. "Why are those men out there?" She nodded in the direction of the men stationed at the trees at each edge of the lawn. "We don't need beaters for clays, so what's their purpose?"

"We've got a dangerous stag loose at the moment. He shouldn't come to an area where shooting is taking place, but we felt the need to cover all possibilities. I'm sure there's nothing to worry about, Miss."

He waited patiently to see her reaction.

"Fair enough." She shrugged and looked down at the gun in her hands before lifting it to her shoulder to test its weight.

"Right, Terrance, Miss Black, you're up first." He retrieved the guns from them all, loaded two of them and handed each back in turn to RJ and Terrance Stocks. They moved into position, RJ on the right side, aiming for the second clay. The others moved back behind the shooters, and two teenage boys discreetly appeared to reload the spare guns as the other two were being fired.

"Ready?" John asked in a deep voice that could be heard over their ear protectors.

Terrance turned his head to look her in the eye and nodded. She returned the nod and focused.

"Pull!" shouted Terrence.

A clay shot out, but RJ ignored it and what happened to it. A split second later, she tracked the next clay with her gun. She pulled the trigger, completely missing her target.

"Don't fret, Miss Black. It takes practice, is all," John reassured her in a respectful yet coddling tone.

"Oh, I'm not worried," she said, not looking at him. "Just getting the feel of it."

Terrance called pull again. RJ breathed, ignoring the world around her and concentrating solely on her clay target. She pulled the trigger, and it smashed to smithereens.

"Well done!"

She passed her gun back to a boy and took the loaded gun from him.

"Thank you."

She took aim and waited for Terrance to give the word, annihilating her clay pigeon yet again. And again.

Her competitive nature didn't allow her to hide her skill and she destroyed every one of her clay pigeons.

"You've done this before," a curious Marshall McDade said as she swapped places with him to walk back towards the gun boys.

She shook her head. "Beginner's luck." As she turned, she noticed Wullie Carstairs watching her from the terrace. She lifted her hand in greeting, and after a pause, he returned the gesture.

McDade and Wainstock began shooting, McDade hitting most of his targets and Wainstock struggling to compete.

Terrance walked over to congratulate her on her shooting. "You did well." He smiled.

"Thank you. I must apologize, though. I wasn't so adept at keeping tabs on your score."

"Oh, you knocked me out of the park, I'm afraid. And I'm pretty good myself. You're rather accomplished for a beginner." He looked at her out of the corner of his eye.

"Well, it's not the first time I've fired a gun."

"Yes, I could see that."

Their conversation was cut short when John lifted his arm as a signal to stop shooting. A car was speeding up the drive. The black Mercedes gave no regard for its paintwork as it careened around the natural bends in the gravel driveway. The group stared in anticipation of its arrival, expecting an eccentric latecomer to their morning shoot.

The Mercedes skidded to a halt in front of the fountain. The driver looked harried and stressed, and before he could get out, the rear passenger door opened. Janice Sullivan shot out of the car. No one was more surprised to see her than RJ. James Sullivan's widow staggered forward, her heels struggling to find purchase in the gravel. She quickly regained her footing, and her composure. "Buchanan! Get out here now. I want answers. You killed my husband! I want to know why."

The driver stood a few feet behind her, red-faced and unsure of what to do. This would not have been in his toolbox of skills that he had picked up on the job, ferrying rich people from A to B. He looked around for help, searching beseechingly for someone who might take the crazy woman off his hands.

The shooters looked at each other in disbelief. They all knew who she was. Even those who hadn't seen her on TV or in a magazine at the latest charity event would have guessed that she was talking, or rather screaming, about James Sullivan.

"Get out here! Get out here, you coward. I want answers." Janice lurched to the side, but her driver caught her before she went down. She sat, her legs twisted underneath her as she clung to him and sobbed.

Wullie Carstairs approached the pair and spoke softly to Janice Sullivan, attempting to defuse the situation and comfort the obviously distressed and very drunk woman.

"He is. He is. I know he's here somewhere," she argued, becoming increasingly distraught. She broke away from the terrified driver and bared her teeth at Carstairs as if ready to pounce. "My husband was killed here. There was no accident. You covered it up, all of you!" She swung an arm to encompass everyone in the vicinity, almost losing her balance again. Her head swiveled and she focused on RJ for the first time, pointing in her direction. "She knows. She knows he was murdered."

All eyes turned on RJ as she stood, open-mouthed, unable to say anything.

Chapter 20

RJ had denied knowing Janice Sullivan, but the group had become suspicious of her, aided in part by her excellent shooting skills. It had been unanimously, and silently, decided that dealing with the crazed woman would be RJ's responsibility, whether she knew Janice or not.

Left with no other choice, RJ managed to get Janice Sullivan back in the Mercedes before getting in her own car and following the widow back to her hotel. The hotel looked nothing less than a castle, with its high-ceilinged rooms, wooden chandeliers, polished floors, and tartan carpeting. Stag heads and claymores decorated the walls. It was the sort of place rich tourists lapped up. Once there, RJ sent the driver away, tipped him generously, and put the poor woman to bed in a sumptuous four poster. Her room was fit for royalty. A framed notice on the wall suggested that it may have provided respite for Bonnie Prince Charlie when he had to flee after the battle of Culloden in 1746. It was hard not to smirk at the sign that probably graced every building over a certain age in the west of Scotland.

When Janice was snoring gently, RJ set a glass of water on the bedside table for when she woke. The combined effects of jet lag and the copious amounts of alcohol had led her to drift off quickly, even though it was just gone noon. Janice would be asleep for a week if there was any justice. No, scrap that. If there was any justice, she would wake up in a few hours with a raging hangover.

RJ left the hotel, exhaling heavily as she did. Just when they felt as though they were getting somewhere, hurricane Janice had to arrive and destroy everything in her path. Not that RJ didn't sympathize but hell . . .

She headed straight to the pub on her way home, downed a much-needed whisky, then went off to tell Stuart about the day's adventures.

"What do we do now?" she asked him. Hopefully, he could see a way out that she couldn't.

"They don't know for sure that you know her," he offered. "She was off her head and clearly distressed."

"You believe that about as much as I do. Carstairs was already suspicious when he found us on the estate. Now he knows he was right to be worried. If Janice hadn't turned up—"

"Yeah, but she did, and now we just have to deal with whatever that means."

RJ shook her head and looked at the ceiling. "We are so close." She knew every crack and imperfection in the sheets of polystyrene. If only she knew as much about the actual case. "I can feel it. We're almost there."

Stuart looked at her with one eyebrow raised. "This doesn't have to be the end. There's more than one way to skin a corrupt gamekeeper. Let's just see what we can figure out. It's not exactly the first setback we've had on this assignment." He kept his tone light.

They war-gamed throughout the afternoon and early evening, trying to figure out what their options were and how they could move forward now that Janice Sullivan had effectively blown their cover.

Chapter 21

"Just what were you thinking?" RJ asked as she paced the floor in Janice Sullivan's generous hotel room the next morning.

Janice lifted her head from the large mahogany desk in the corner and stared at RJ through gritty eyes. "I wasn't. I wasn't thinking. Isn't that obvious?"

She'd managed to get herself up and had taken a half-hearted shower but hadn't made it as far as getting dressed or leaving the room. A barely touched bowl of porridge sat on a tray in front of her, and she pushed it away ineffectually. The sleeve of her plush, white robe fell in the bowl as she waved it off with her hand.

"Do you even realize what you've done?" RJ demanded. She towered over Janice, hands on her hips, anger radiating from every pore.

Janice didn't answer. Her head remained on the desk and a low moan erupted from somewhere under the mass of tangled hair.

"You've put the whole assignment in jeopardy, completely blown our cover to the people we were trying to investigate. You've compromised our ability to uncover the truth. Now that these people know we're investigating them, they're going to cover their tracks even more carefully." RJ through her hands up in frustration. "Why the hell did you come here?"

Janice began to sob. The only other sound in the room was RJ's harsh and labored breathing.

She tried to have more sympathy for the woman, but damn it, her job was to find out what had happened to James Sullivan, not babysit his widow or treat her with kid gloves when she had just jeopardized the whole mission.

"I'm sorry, I just . . ." Janice attempted between sobs.

RJ tried to rein in her anger, but it wasn't easy.

"It's just, nothing's happening. You haven't found anything."

"You haven't given us any time. The investigation is progressing, or it had been until you arrived. We can't relay every tiny detail as we find it. If you had just waited . . ." RJ snapped at her in frustration. Ever since the drunk driver had caused her parents' deaths, she abhorred drunks, abhorred people who relinquished their control over their actions.

Janice lifted her head with difficulty and scooted back in her chair to look at RJ. Some of her hair was plastered to her face, the rest a chaotic mess. She peered at RJ through slatted eyes. "Maybe it all needed to come out. Have you thought of that?"

"No. It didn't need to come out. We were making progress and would have been able to find out more if you hadn't just dropped in and arsed it all up."

"I'm fed up with all these secrets and lies. I just want to know what happened. I want my James back."

The tears started again, flowing silently and unapologetically down Janice's face. She stared at RJ, who returned the look, neither willing to submit.

RJ ground her teeth. After a long, few minutes, Janice looked away.

"My brother hasn't told you everything. He's trying to protect himself and his campaign. He says he's trying to project James's memory, but that's crap. He's trying to save his own skin. Doesn't want the negative publicity. Sure, he cared about James and he cares about me, but he cares about Brand Kowalski more."

"Have you got any idea what he isn't telling us?" RJ probed. She unfolded her arms and pulled a chair over to sit close to Janice. "If we had known the whole story at the start, we might have been much further in the investigation now. Do you realize that? If you and your brother want to find out the truth, you've got a duty to tell us everything, even if you think it has no bearing on the case. It's up to us to determine that."

Janice pulled at the dried porridge on the end of her sleeve, loosening a thread which she pulled free and twisted around her middle finger, watching until the tip turned purple. She unwound the thread and stared at the line where it had cut into her skin. Still, she refused to meet RJ's eye.

"James liked to hunt," she said quietly.

"We know that."

Janice sighed deeply into her bathrobe. "Well, James liked hunting. He hunted all over the world. It was his thing, his hobby. A way for him to de-stress and get away from it all. He was an important man under a lot of stress. He needed to unwind. Anyone could understand that. So, he hunted. He spent his entire life working hard for his money, so he made sure he always got the best, paid for the best products and services available. Money wasn't an issue, you see." She took a breath and blew it out between her teeth, suddenly reticent to go on.

"And?" RJ prompted.

"He wasn't a trophy hunter, not in the traditional sense. He'd never bring his kills home."

RJ scooted forward in her seat as understanding dawned. "Those statues in your garden—the giraffe, the elephant—those were his trophies, weren't they?"

"Yes," Janice admitted and cast her gaze out of the window. "He liked to hunt big game, has for years. We've kept it quiet so as not to affect his businesses or Michael's career. You've seen the kind of thing I mean. These things go viral all over the world. People get villainized. James wasn't a bad person. He wasn't hurting anyone. So, he was careful; he never even took a photograph of his kills."

RJ tried to disguise the disgust growing in her gut.

"And you think this might have something to do with James's death?"

"It's possible. Some sort of environmental nut may have found out and taken their revenge." She turned to look at RJ. "It's an angle you should look into. These people don't understand the kind of pressure men like my husband are under. Maybe they aren't content with ruining careers and lives anymore. They might have stepped up their attacks." It was clear Janice actually believed what she was saying justified her husband's little hobby.

"With respect, Mrs. Sullivan. I don't think I'll personally be looking into anything now that you've dropped this bomb on the investigation." RJ stood up and walked to the window, looking down at the tourists enjoying the breeze in the hotel gardens, the morning already hot. She sighed. "Has there been any indication that anyone found out about the big game hunting?"

"No. Not to my knowledge. James has always gotten hate mail or threats because he hunts and is in the public eye, but nothing to suggest that anyone knew he was hunting anything other than the regular deer and pigs."

RJ turned to look at her. "Then what makes you think it has anything to do with his death?"

"I'm not saying it does, just that it might. I don't know. I just want everything out in the open. I want to find out what happened. You lot need as much information as possible to do that. No secrets. Plus, he was killed when he was hunting . . ."

RJ tried to think. "There's a mad stag on the estate at the moment. Perhaps that's what killed him. Poetic justice, so to speak. The Buchanans would certainly want to keep that quiet. It could be why they're so keen to talk about it. A double bluff," she said in a low breath to herself.

"You don't approve." Janice looked dejected. "I knew there was a risk in telling you, but I had to."

"Approve?"

"Of James's hobby."

"Whether I approve of not has no bearing on the case," RJ said, voice hard as she looked away. She couldn't get involved in an ethical discussion.

She rubbed her face with both hands, and some of the sunscreen that she'd never imagined she'd need in Scotland got into her eye. RJ grabbed a tissue from the box on the desk and dabbed at her stinging and watering eyes. Her mascara came off, and she wiped carefully underneath her lashes. Discarding the tissue in the bin gave her some time to think.

"Look, I'll need to talk to my bosses, but it's likely I'll get pulled off the case. We'll regroup and decide on the next steps. I'll pass on all the information you just gave me. That's all I can do. I'm really sorry, but if you hadn't disrupted the investigation, hadn't made such a scene on Buchanan property, then . . ." She shrugged and raised her eyes to the ceiling.

"I know, I know that. Don't you think . . . I'm just so angry and no one is telling me anything. I'm so lost and I don't know what to do." Janice's voice broke as she started sobbing again.

"Well, you're certainly not going to find the answer at the bottom of a bottle," RJ told her gently. "Just go home, Janice. Go home and be with family and friends. This isn't helping, and it certainly isn't helping you find the answers you want. I get it, believe me I do. It's not fair that the person you loved was snatched away from you. You feel like your heart is being ripped to pieces and there's nothing you can do. I get it." She laid her hand over Janice's. "But leave this to us, okay?"

Janice nodded through her tears. There was nothing more RJ could do but leave.

She sat in her car with the windows down as she waited for the interior to cool down. Janice had ruined everything in one fell, drunken, swoop. She laid her head back against the headrest and closed her eyes. It was over. Although it was clear that it wasn't her fault, she still felt a sense of failure.

Once the car had sufficiently cooled down, she closed the windows and drove off with the air conditioning on. She pulled over to the side of the road once out of town, keeping the engine running for the air con. Even though she had stopped in a quiet area, she couldn't risk anyone overhearing her conversation by opening the windows. She took out her phone to call in and explain the problem to headquarters, but the phone rang in her hand before she got the chance. Stuart's name flashed on the caller ID.

"It's human, the bone you found, it's definitely human," he began without preamble. She could hear his sigh as she imagined his shoulders drooping down in defeat.

RJ could taste blood again from inside her mouth where she'd been worrying her cheek. "Is it him? Is it Sullivan?"

"We're still waiting for the DNA testing. But I'd say there's a high chance."

So close. They were so close to discovering what really happened to James Sullivan, but Janice just had to come along and ruin it all. Now, they might never find out. Janice's behavior had given those involved a warning to bury their tracks even deeper.

RJ dialed in to HQ, defeated.

Macey, her handler for this assignment, was nonplussed. "She did what?" There was a pause. "You'll need to come in. There's no way you could talk your way out of that. I'll start organizing an alternative team right away. Pack up your things and leave right away. I'll organize transport back when you're on the road. The sooner you get out of there, the better."

"I agree. If they see us again, it'll only make them more suspicious and cautious. We've tried to figure a way around it, but we see no other choice. I'm just hoping this hasn't blown the whole case."

"Only time will tell. Good job on your progress so far. I mean it. You've done well."

"Thanks, Macey," she said before hanging up. She sent a text to Stuart.

Start packing, we're being pulled out.

Checking her mirrors, she pulled back onto the road and headed towards the village for the last time.

As she pulled through the gate at the side of the pub, she saw Kirsty waiting for her.

"No school today?" RJ asked her when she got out of the car.

"Strike," the girl explained. "My mum said teachers don't get paid enough so they have to not go to school today. It means we don't have to, either."

"No, I'm quite sure they don't get paid enough. No brothers to play with today?"

"They've gone off to catch the cat."

"Oh no, has Socks gone missing?" asked RJ, genuinely worried for the friendly little ball of fluff.

Kirsty looked at her like she was crazy and shook her head. "Up in the hills," she explained as if that would tell RJ everything she needed to know.

"I hope they're not going after wildcats. They're endangered—there are hardly any of them left, I mean. I'd imagine they can be quite vicious, too. Does your mum know what they're up to?"

Kirsty shook her head. "What's a wildcat?"

RJ's eyes grew wide as it all fell into place. She turned from Kirsty and raced up the steps to the cabin, leaving the car door wide open. She rushed in to find Stuart folding the last of his clothes in his black hold-all.

"We have to go," she gasped, suddenly out of breath despite the lack of real exertion.

"Yeah, I'm just finishing up." He looked up at her, and she saw his expression change from annoyance to concern as his eyes landed on hers. "What's the rush?"

"No, I mean we have to go now. I know what happened. The twins could be in danger. Hurry."

Chapter 22

Stuart jumped up from the bed, grimacing as he put his weight on his sore ankle. "Shit, ow . . . what is it?" he asked through gritted teeth.

"Big game hunting. It's not a rogue stag they've got on the loose, it's a big cat."

"Holy shit." Stuart hobbled over to his bag. "And you say the boys are out there looking for it?"

He rummaged about and took out a pistol.

"Got one of those for me?"

He shook his head. "Sorry."

"This'll have to do then." She pulled out her knife and tested the tip against her finger, staring at it disconcertedly before slotting it back in her ankle strap.

She rushed down the stairs to the car with Stuart hobbling behind as fast as he could. "You go," he shouted. "I'll take the car".

RJ ran on. There was no way Stuart would have managed to keep up. Also, he could cover more ground with the car. Her advantage was that she was on foot just as the boys were, so she might be able to find them sooner.

She ran down the road and squirmed through the fence. Her foot caught the wire and almost sent her sprawling, but she caught herself in time and pulled it through. Looking at the road ahead, she decided it was the least likely route the boys would have taken. Instead, she ran up the side of the hill to try and get a better perspective on where they might have headed. Her heart pounded in her chest from fear of what she might be too late to prevent.

#

The wheels spun in the gravel as Stuart gunned the car down the side of the pub and onto the road, narrowly missing a little old granny and her tartan shopping trolley who jumped out of the way, quicker on her feet than she likely had been in years. She stood, shaking her fist in the air at the car as it disappeared down the road.

Once he'd reached the gates to the estate, Stuart jumped out and pressed the intercom.

A gruff male voice answered. "Yes?"

"There are two ten-year-old boys loose on the estate. They've gone to look for the cat. Jesus Christ, get everybody out looking for them and let me through."

There was a long pause on the other end during which Stuart could hear heavy breathing.

“God help us,” came a quiet voice before the gates swung open.

Stuart rushed back to the car, spinning the wheels as he drove through. He saw RJ at the crest of the hill, scanning the landscape, and ploughed on to cover more ground than she could. It was unlikely that the boys would stick to the road, but if he could just spot them . . . He’d worry about what he could do after that.

#

RJ could see no sign of the boys. She looked back to the forest and wondered if they could possibly be in there. She tried to put herself in the mind of a ten-year-old boy. Where would he look? Not in the trees. They’d be ranging over the hills. Hoping she was right, she ran on, aiming for the next hill, stopping every few minutes to look in all directions. She’d decided against shouting because they’d likely go to ground if they knew someone was looking for them. Her—and their—only chance was to find them.

Her phone buzzed in her pocket and she took it out.

“I’m in,” Stuart said. “Any sign?”

"Nothing. They must've come in through the trees at the back of the pub but where they went after that . . ."

"Any idea what we're dealing with here?"

"Other than a huge feline, not a clue." Their lack of information frustrated her. "Orange, yellow, black, brown. Could be anything. Whatever it is, it's big enough to pay a lot of money to kill. Big enough to kill a grown man," she added. "And it could be anywhere. With any luck, it'll be nowhere near here. If we'd had more time after figuring it out, we could've found out more about how to find it."

"Presumably the gamekeepers know that and they haven't managed to find it yet," he pointed out. "Speaking of which, any sign of them yet?"

"Nothing," RJ replied. "They'll come. They can't risk two little boys being torn apart. It would be a bit harder to cover up than before."

#

She watched from the mouth of her cave as the two stalked about in the grass below. She'd been woken from her sleep by the noise they made. Tilting her head to the side, she considered their value and whether they were a threat. If they came any closer, she'd take action. For now, she was content just to watch them, ready to pounce. She'd eaten recently, so she wasn't hungry, but her instincts gave her a desire to attack what looked like easy prey.

#

The twins plodded on through the long grass that alternated between tickling their shins and scratching them.

"This is hopeless. There's no cat," one of them complained. If truth be told, he was more than a little scared, but didn't want to show it to his brother, who had always been the more adventurous of the two.

"Aye, there is, we just have to find it," his brother replied, whacking at the grass with a stick he'd found amongst the trees. Flies scattered from their perches on the plants to find more animal waste to consume.

"We'll need to come back another day. Mam will be looking for us for our tea soon."

"One more minute. Look." He pointed up the hill and unknowingly in the direction of the hidden cave. "We'll get to the top and have a look. If we can't see it from up there, we'll go home, come back on Saturday when we've got more time. If we can't see it, then maybe we can go looking for snakes. Alfie Edwards says he found one in the rocks near that cliff over there."

"Aye, okay," the first reluctantly agreed, keen to get back to the safety of their pub and even their annoying little sister. "But I wouldn't believe anything Alfie Edwards says. He talks pish and you know it. If he did find something, they were probably just slow worms. They're no snakes, you know," he told his brother with a grimace.

They stood, looking all the while like little old men, their hands on their hips as they tried to catch their breath before tackling their last summit.

"Yeah, well, just imagine telling him and everyone else at school when we find the cat."

The first twin didn't want to think about the possibility of finding the cat but traipsed on after his brother, in the hope that they'd soon be heading home, exhausted and empty-handed but in one piece.

#

RJ slowed and caught her breath. She was fit but not up to fell running like this. Maybe the panic was starting to set in. Logically, she knew that both she and Stuart had been on this land twice and hadn't come across anything, so the likelihood that the boys would stumble upon the big cat was small, but what if they did find what they were looking for . . . or what if it found them?

She looked across the green countryside. The sheep were spread out and grazing, which could only be a good sign. There were no little red heads bobbing among them. What she could see was Stuart's car off in the distance and a Land Rover coming from the other direction, dust kicking up from the tires.

She turned back and shielded the sun from her eyes. Movement down by the water of the estate's reservoir caught her eye, and she tried to focus on the dark shadow.

"Damn it," she muttered in exasperation. It wasn't them, just a trick of the light from a lonely cloud floating overhead. She stood at the top of the hill and slowly rotated three-hundred-and-sixty degrees, searching out over the hills and glens below. All that was here, or all she could see, were sheep. Just sheep and more sheep; lambs almost the size of their mothers, all of their wool recently shorn off. She took a breath, then repeated the process. Nothing. The boys weren't here, perhaps they never had been or perhaps they had come and gone. Gone under their own stead or . . .

It didn't bear thinking about.

#

Stuart saw the dust from the vehicle coming his way before the Land Rover crested the hill. Both cars stopped, facing each other. Wullie Carstairs and Stuart locked eyes. Anger mixed with terror emanated from the older man's eyes.

"Just what are you doing here?" the gamekeeper asked before he had fully extracted himself from the car.

"Looking for the boys. I told you. We have to find them before something else does."

"That's no' what I meant, and you know it," Carstairs growled at him.

"We're private investigators, hired to look into James Sullivan's death. None of that matters now. We have to find the boys."

Carstairs gave a grim nod. "The rest of the boys are checking other areas; I've got three other keepers today. They all know what's what. We'll find them." His voice wavered over the last statement. "Get in, that car's useless off road."

Stuart got in the Land Rover and listened to the agitated radio chatter that pierced the air as reports from the other gamekeepers came through.

"Nothing by Smith's brook."

"No sightings from Giant's tor."

Carstairs picked up the radio. "Mrs. Webster, you head down to the pub. Keep an eye out and let us know if the boys return."

"Yes, Mr. Carstairs."

"And Betty . . . don't give anything away."

He put the radio down and grabbed the gear stick in one swift move. The car lurched forward as it pulled off the road and started the climb around the side of a hill, leaning over to the side and putting the driver's side higher than the passenger.

"That your wife up there?" Carstairs nodded towards RJ's solitary figure high on a hill ahead.

"Yes. She figured it out and we came after the boys."

"If she figured it out, then she should be smart enough to know that being out in the open like that is stupid and reckless. I wouldn't let my wife do something like that."

"We didn't have much choice," Stuart snapped back. "And she's not really my wife."

"Even so, bloody stupid thing to do."

The car bumped over rocks and ruts, Carstairs paying no heed to any attempt to soften the ride, caring only about covering ground and fast.

"There's been carcasses found over a huge area, so we can't pinpoint her location. She always seems one step ahead of us," he explained reluctantly.

"She?"

"Aye, she. We're lucky it's a she. Males roam a far greater area and are bigger."

"What exactly are we dealing with here?" Stuart asked.

"A black panther," Carstairs told him. "A fully grown and pissed off black panther. A jaguar, to be precise. Pure, solid muscle.

#

RJ wiped the sweat out of her eyes. Her shirt was sticking to her back and a dribble of moisture ran down between her shoulder blades. *Let's think about this logically. Two small boys wouldn't have hiked far, they'd be dilly-dallying, meandering over the land, exploring nooks and crannies. They shouldn't be this far in.* In her haste to cover ground and get to a higher point, she must have come too far.

RJ turned back the way she had come, aiming for the trees in the distance. The trees where the boys had likely come through at the start of their adventure. They must be somewhere between there and here. She carefully made her way down the slope. The last thing she needed was to injure herself like Stuart had.

At the bottom, she started to run across the grass, scattering the sheep that grazed on the juicy green shoots. Over a hillock and round a pile of rocks she ran, constantly looking around, searching for the two little boys who could be in grave danger.

She took out her phone and dialed Stuart's number. "I've found them," she told him, staring up at the figures of the twins as they climbed the hill in front of her.

Chapter 23

She climbed slowly, so as not to alert the boys and frighten them off. The last thing she wanted, now that she had finally found them, was for them to take flight and have her chase them all over again.

They disappeared out of sight over the top of the hill, and she began to crawl upwards on her hands, pulling herself up over moss-covered rocks, rabbit holes that had long since held any animals, and jaggy nettles that pricked at her hands with what should have been a warm spiky sensation that grew with each second. She was oblivious to it all; the only thing she was aware of was her need to get to the boys.

She could hear them chattering away up ahead.

"Right, nothing. I told you. Come on. Home."

"Aye, fine. Just a minute, though. Here." He pulled out a squashed jam sandwich wrapped in cling film, unwrapped it, tore it in half and offered it to his brother.

"How'd you no' tell me you had that before? I'm starving."

The boy shrugged and chewed on his sandwich, looking out over the expanse of the estate below them. Luckily, the incline was too steep on the side of the hill for them to notice RJ making her way towards them, unless they decided to get close to the edge and peer directly over.

"We need a plan," the adventurous one stated.

"Aye."

"We'll go to the library after school, find out more about them and where they like to live and what they like to eat. Then we'll be able to find it."

"Well, they don't like to live in bloody Scotland."

"Aye, well . . . I mean up trees, near water. That sort of stuff."

"We don't even know what it is," the more-timid one reasoned. He sighed dramatically. His legs were sore and he could feel his cheeks starting to burn. Their mum wasn't going to be happy that they'd forgotten to put their sunscreen on before leaving for the afternoon. Hell, if Mum was going to be upset over that, then she'd be raging that they'd gone off on the estate and absolutely livid that they were hunting a big wild cat.

"You know that this might be a load of rubbish, don't you? There might be nothing up here." He secretly hoped this was the case. A paltry stick between the two of them wasn't much defense against a wild animal.

A grunt behind them made them freeze in mid-bite.

"What was that?" The braver twin suddenly grasped at the hand of his brother.

Slowly, they turned round, shaking like the last quivering leaves left on a nearly naked tree.

The jaguar sat a good ten meters away, sunlight bouncing off her luxurious coat, her spots and rosettes shining through her dark fur. She tilted her head to the side, studying the curious little creatures in front of her. Her mouth was partially open, allowing them to see her pink tongue and the intimidating canines on her lower jaw.

As the brave twin felt the warmth of his bladder releasing down his leg, he suddenly regretted his idea to come looking for the animal that now sat in front of him. He gripped his brother tighter and let out a strangled squeak.

"Don't run, don't move," his brother told him. The acrid tang of urine that emanated from his brother made him realize that he had to take charge. He pushed the fear down and squeezed his twin's hand to let him know he was there and that he'd make it all right . . . somehow.

RJ could no longer hear the boys and hoped they hadn't decided to go off down the other side. She picked up her pace, her stinging hands scraping painfully on the rocks. She looked behind her. There was no sign of Stuart or the Land Rover. Perhaps the boys had seen one of the cars and gotten spooked. When she peeked over the hill, she saw the boys' upper bodies. They seemed to be frozen in place, unable to move.

Damn it, she didn't like the look of this. Ducking back down, she reached for the knife in her ankle strap. She took a deep breath and blew it out between her teeth. Gripping the knife in her fist, she gently raised herself up to survey the scene.

The boys were still in place. Beyond them, a muscular black head turned her way. The jaguar seemed perfectly relaxed, pondering the scene. RJ could see the boys shaking uncontrollably, unsure of what to do next, caught like rabbits in the headlights of the jaguar's gaze. They were cognizant enough to know that if they tried to run, they wouldn't stand a chance against the muscular beast who was, so obviously, the one in control of the situation.

RJ slowly raised herself to her feet, keeping low to appear as less of a threat, but ready to react when the need arose. She shuffled through the grass and spoke in a low voice, as much not to spook the animal as to not spook the boys.

"'S'alright, boys. You're going to be okay. This is fine, don't worry. We're going to get you out of this. Everything is going to be fine."

The boys stared straight ahead but the one nearest to her gave an almost imperceptible nod. They didn't seem surprised to see her, or even relieved at all that someone else was there. The unpredictability of people in stressful situations was a threat to all of their safety. Children, who generally possessed less self-control, were all the more unpredictable. If there was ever a situation that was not ideal, it was this one.

"Don't make any sudden moves, okay?" she told them in a calm voice that sounded confident but was anything but. "Now, I'm just going to move slowly . . ."

The jaguar jerked her head at a sound only audible to her, and the world stood still. RJ stopped mid-step and held her breath.

The jaguar looked back at them, its golden eyes shining with a predatory self-assurance.

RJ placed her foot tentatively on the grass, her eyes never leaving the cat's for a second. When there were no further changes in movement, RJ continued her slow shuffle towards the terrified boys, all the while talking to them in soft tones. Her hand felt slick on the hilt of the knife. She prayed she'd have the strength to use it effectively against what was basically a wall of muscle that had been honed over thousands of years to become a highly efficient killing machine. She'd try and go for the neck—if she had any choice in the matter. She knew nothing about animal anatomy, but assumed it would be the most vulnerable area. If she could just keep it busy for long enough, hold its attention. The odds weren't in her favor, and yet she continued on until she stood in front of the twins, providing them with a poor defensive barrier.

The jaguar looked on, then stood up, stretching its hind legs. RJ watched in amazement at the similarity of this action to an ordinary everyday feline. It began to pace along the rocky ledge, drawing RJ's attention to the shallow cave behind it.

We've walked right into its lair, RJ realized. Both she and Stuart had walked close by each time they'd hiked through the estate before and had seen no sign of it. So why now? Why had it decided to show itself now? RJ's thoughts went to the boys behind her. Easy and juicy targets to the jaguar.

A voice, barely above a whisper came from behind her. "What do we do now?"

"I don't know . . . I guess we wait for help and try not to aggravate it."

"I want my mum," came a whimper from the other side.

"It'll be okay, boys. I'm not going to let anything happen to you," RJ muttered as she watched the jaguar walk to and fro, its movements increasingly impatient. Her instinct was to turn sideways, to present less of a target and set up a fighting stance, but she had to provide as wide a shield as possible for the twins behind her. She raised her arms out to the side in a stance not unlike a ballet dancer, trying to make herself look bigger and more intimidating to the beast. It went against what every cell in her body was screaming at her to do.

The jaguar stopped again and lifted its head as if to scent the air. Soon after, RJ heard what the cat must have heard: the rumble of an engine coming closer. It sat back down on the rock and waited.

"Hear that, boys? Help is on its way. We're going to get you out of here soon."

The boy over her right shoulder started to sniff, holding back tears that threatened to spill over and consume him.

"We're all right, we're all right, we're all right, we're all right," came his brother's whispered response.

RJ slowly swapped her knife to her other hand and wiped her palm on her shorts. Any movement was a risk, but she needed a firm grip. It wasn't much of a weapon, and it looked like the jaguar knew that as it stood watching them. It was toying with them, like a domestic pet tormenting a mouse.

Hurry. RJ willed the arrival of Stuart or the Land Rover that was roaming the estate. Her prayers were answered when the Land Rover pulled up parallel to them on the slope behind her.

Carstairs leveled a shotgun on the jaguar as Stuart crept out of the passenger side and around the back of the car. "Okay, boys, what you're going to do is calmly and slowly turn around, and then very carefully walk towards me."

The jaguar looked on. RJ was amazed that it hadn't run in fear when the car pulled up. That wasn't a good sign.

"I'll stay here until you get the boys in the car," she said, angling her head slightly over her shoulder so Stuart could hear her.

He hesitated. It made sense. Provide a target for the jaguar while the boys got out of range, but

Stuart had a sense of loyalty towards his colleague and now friend. "Okay," he breathed, unsure how he could even consider the idea.

"I can't," one of the boys said in a scared voice.

"You can," RJ, Stuart, and his brother told him in unison.

Stuart leaned forward and held out his hand. "Come on now."

The twin on the left gently tugged at his brother's sleeve and they slowly swiveled round, eyes closed and gulping in unison.

Stuart nodded and let out a breath. "Come forward, just slowly now and careful where you put your feet. Whatever you do, don't stumble."

The terrified boy with the wet patch down the front of his shorts opened his eyes wide in terror and the realization of what would likely happen if one of them were to fall.

"We can do this. We'll do it together," his brother told him.

Stuart focused on the boys and their slow progress towards him, afraid to look up at the jaguar and his partner that stood between them.

The twins' passage was excruciatingly slow. Stuart inched forward, wanting to envelop them in his arms but knowing that was impossible. His fingers touched their hands before he moved forward to provide another line of defense. They moved tightly as a unit to the other side of the car, then Stuart pushed them in, in quick succession, before shutting the door.

The jaguar had watched the proceedings with an air of bemused boredom, but snapped her head up at the slam of the door.

"They're safe, your turn," Stuart told RJ.

RJ's legs felt like they could give way and betray her at any moment. She swallowed and took a step backwards. Unlike the boys who'd had something between themselves and the jaguar, RJ was too exposed to turn away and had little choice but to back away, her eyes on the danger ahead.

As she took another step back, her heel tipped too far over the edge of a rabbit hole. She went down, her arms cart-wheeling out as she instinctively tried to right herself. As she went down, she saw the jaguar leap through the air towards her.

Chapter 24

The graceful leap through the air would have been impressive had RJ witnessed it from afar and not been the intended target of the powerful black beast. One huge bound from a stationary position saw the jaguar soar over a distance of five meters to land neatly on top of her target.

RJ threw her hands up to protect herself and readied her knife as she went down, watching the cat sail towards her. She didn't hear the bang from behind her, was aware of nothing except the weight of the jaguar on top of her chest as she was thrown down on the ground.

The heavy body pressed down on her torso, suffocating her and filling her with panic. Its teeth on her neck were unmoving. She stayed still, afraid to move, to do anything that might antagonize it.

Suddenly, the weight was pulled from her and she could breathe again. She stayed down and gulped in lungful after lungful of air, her heart beating wildly.

Stuart appeared in her field of vision and looked down at her; Wullie Carstairs soon joined him. RJ stared up at the two men. She made no attempt to control her breathing or slow her heart rate. She just lay there, trying to process what had just happened.

"You look like you've just seen a ghost," Stuart said.

"Yeah, my own. I don't want to repeat that ever again," she hissed out between breaths.

She tried to sit up on her elbows, but Stuart gently pushed her back down again. "Just rest a minute, wait until your heart rate calms down. You need to stop it pumping so hard."

"I'm okay," she insisted and then turned to see his hand, which rested very close to a mass of red flesh and blood where she'd expected to see her shoulder. Her vision turned gray and fuzzy, everything sounded far away as if she was caught in a fog, and she lost herself to the darkness.

When she awoke, she was on her side, with a rolled-up shirt under her head. "What happened?" she managed.

"You blacked out. You're okay. Just . . . don't look at it again."

"I don't plan on it," she told him dryly.

"Thanks to Wullie here, that's all the damage you got."

RJ raised an eyebrow. So, it was Wullie now, was it? They were on a first name basis.

"I was in the back of the car with the two boys, trying to keep them down and protect them from seeing . . . well. Anyway, so I was looking after the boys who were huddled down, terrified. We're lucky that Wullie is such a good shot."

RJ smiled weakly at Wullie Carstairs.

"This has to end now," he said grimly. "Too many people have gotten hurt, and if anything had happened to those boys—" Wullie broke off and stared off into the distance.

No one said anything for a long time.

"Right." Wullie stalked back to his car and retrieved the radio. He thumbed the talk button. Static crackled through the speaker. "I need a car up at Acre's Ridge. Samuel, you're to take the boys home. Tam, bring another car up. Bring the big first-aid kit with you. You'll be retrieving a carcass when you get here, so bring John up with you, too."

RJ eased herself up to sitting position. She looked back at the car. Two little boys with eyes the size of dinner plates stared out of the back window.

"You can't keep this a secret anymore, not now."

"You really think anyone will believe those two?" Wullie asked her.

"You can't just ignore it. Their mother will have to be told. They'll need help through it."

Wullie Carstairs stared at her, looking both angry and exasperated. He stalked back to the car. "Right, lads. When you go home, not a word to your mum about what really happened, eh?"

They nodded quickly at him, faces white with fear.

He sighed and looked back at the jaguar that lay dead and bloodied on the hill. "I'll be down tonight to talk to your mum. I'll tell her everything. For just now, though, you need to keep your mouths shut. Do you understand?"

They nodded again, clearly ready to agree to anything in that moment.

RJ could only wonder how their young minds were processing this crazily unique situation. Goodness knows her own was having trouble, so they must have been all over the place.

The engine of a car came gradually closer. Another Land Rover pulled up, and a tall man, presumably Samuel due to the absence of a first-aid kit and dressed in the same manner as Carstairs, got out. The blood drained from his face and he looked as shell-shocked as the twins.

Wullie nodded in greeting, but Samuel was oblivious as he looked at RJ's shoulder, then over it at the jaguar that lay dead on the ground.

"Samuel, take them back down. Tell their mum we had to rescue them from the rogue stag. That'll explain their reactions, for now anyway." He turned to the boys in the car and opened the door. As they hopped out, he stopped them before they went to Samuel, laying a hand on each twin's arm. "Remember what I said boys. Not a word."

"Yes, Mr. Carstairs," they answered earnestly in unison.

He continued to look in their eyes for a minute before ushering them off to Samuel and their ride home.

The three people left on the hill watched the car until it disappeared out of sight, knowing, each one of them, that it could have ended very differently.

"Right, get in then," Carstairs told them as he got into the driver's seat of the old, beat-up Land Rover.

Stuart held out his hand and helped RJ to her feet. "Okay?"

"Yep, okay." She got into the front seat, ignoring the seatbelt and preparing to hold out her good arm against the dash for when they went over any bumps.

"I'll try to take it as easy as I can," Carstairs promised, looking directly at the red slashes on her shoulder that were dripping fresh blood onto the upholstery, turning it crimson.

Carstairs was good to his word, driving slowly around dips and rocks, taking his time on the descent down the hill. He slowed even further when they approached an oncoming ATV. He rolled down his window and nodded at the driver, who mirrored the action, unsmiling. The driver handed over a hold-all that Carstairs set on his lap before driving off down the road again.

The adrenaline that had been coursing through RJ's veins started to wear off in direct correlation with the increasing pain she now noticed in her arm and shoulder. She winced and looked at the bag on Carstairs's lap. "That's a pretty big first-aid kit."

"It's a pretty big estate, and a working farm, if you haven't noticed. Someone could get hurt and we're miles from help out here."

"What have you got in there?" Stuart asked, leaning over from the back seat.

"Everything you'll need, except the tetanus jab. There's even a suture kit . . . but the most I've ever done before was sliced fingers." He looked out of the window and blew out a breath, his mouth forming a perfect O.

"No worries about that. I'll handle it," Stuart said as if sewing up slashed shoulders was an everyday occurrence for him.

"You two, you're not really private detectives, are you? I figure PIs would've gotten the police involved by now, or at the very least insisted on a doctor."

"No," RJ answered.

"I don't suppose you're going to tell me who you are?"

"No," RJ said and looked out of her window, watching the green grass roll by.

"I figured you weren't, not after . . ." He waved vaguely in the direction of her injury. "Most people would have panicked or insisted on phoning 999. Not you two, though. It makes sense. I couldn't see the Sullivan widow hiring any old private investigation firm."

"She didn't hire us." It was the only thing RJ conceded, but she felt no danger in letting him know.

"Oh." His expression fell even more than it had before. The lines on his face were deeper, his skin sallower than when they had first seen him. He looked like a broken man. He sighed repeatedly, as if he had a war waging within himself.

"There are things you have to understand."

"Two people are dead. Now we know why. What's left to understand?"

"It's not as simple as that. I'll explain everything, but I need to show you something first."

They drove up to the house, skirting around the edge of the building and driving past it.

"Where are you taking us?" RJ asked, suddenly wary. She had no idea where her knife was. She must have dropped it either in the scuffle with the jaguar or afterwards in the confusion of her injury.

"I just need . . . You won't understand until I show you. It's not what you think. You can't even begin to imagine what it's been like. No one can, except those of us who work here. You have to see it."

They trundled on for what must have been two miles or more, eventually coming to a stop outside a large gray barn, squatting in a flat valley that had been carved out by an immense body of ice hundreds of thousands of years previously. The barn—or maybe it was a shed—looked newer than she would have expected a building on a farm or estate such as this to be. Breeze blocks towered out of the ground for about fifteen feet and stopped where the curved steel roof started arcing up to the sky like a depressingly mundane rainbow. Nothing in its surrounds or on the building itself gave any clues as to its purpose.

They got out of the car, with RJ moving slower than the others. Tears pricked at her eyes as she gently unfolded herself from the passenger seat. There was time for a quick glance between her and Stuart before they followed Carstairs up to the door in the center of the structure. The glance told her all she had to know. *What have we got to lose?*

Carstairs keyed a number into an electronic keypad that seemed incongruous with the country building, then took a key from his pocket and turned it in the lock under the pad. "Double entry system," he explained, without actually explaining anything at all, and then walked through, expecting them to follow.

She glanced at Stuart again. He shrugged and followed him through. Having little other choice, RJ did the same. It occurred to her they were an unlikely bunch: Stuart with his scabbed face and pronounced limp, her with her shoulder ripped open, and Carstairs the haggard gamekeeper. It was like something out of a horror movie or a haunted house, one of those ones where made-up, scary characters jump out from the dark corners, terrifying willing patrons.

Her hand felt empty without her knife, but she assumed Stuart still had his gun. She wasn't afraid, just wary. If Carstairs had wanted to kill them, he could have easily taken them out earlier. There was no reason to give her access to first aid if they were going to be dead soon. Even so, she was on her guard, ready to fight if needed.

A corridor ran tunnel-like to a door at the end. The walls were made of the same rough breeze block of the walls outside. Carstairs opened the door with another key, lighting the lock with a tiny torch on his key ring.

They couldn't see anything as they walked into the dark, but the smell was overpowering. Straw and the stench of animal feces, mostly, along with something else RJ didn't recognize.

"I'll just get the light," Carstairs said. They heard him shuffle away, saw the tiny beam of light from his torch on the floor, and then there was the click of a switch before the light illuminated the room. It took a second for RJ's eyes to adjust to the bright light. When they did, she was completely blown away. It was not at all what she'd been expecting. She looked at Stuart to see his mouth hanging open in wonder.

"Holy shitballs," he said to no one in particular.

Chapter 25

Cages lined the walls like kennels—or perhaps it was more accurate to think of them as pens—enclosed with concrete blocks and wire mesh on each of the walls in front. The cages ran up the sides, reaching right to the far wall, and formed two lines up the middle of the building. The roaring and growling started as soon as the lights came on, growing in intensity as the animals fed from each other's apprehension. No good ever came from the presence of the humans or the lights, except the sustenance that failed to keep them truly nourished in either body or soul.

RJ walked up to the first pen, knowing what she would find but still needing the confirmation that seeing it with her own eyes gave her. Shriveled in a corner at the back sat a female lion. The pen was separated by a wall of bars, an open door leading to the mirror image of the cell she was in. Her fur was dull and thin and her abdomen painfully extended. She bared her teeth in a show of defiance, but RJ doubted the feline would have the energy to even try to defend herself if the need arose. Tears burned the back of her eyes and she had to force herself to move on.

The next pen held a jaguar nursing four little cubs. All five cats looked much healthier than the lion. The mother looked at RJ with interest but gave no other indications of her feelings towards the situation. Her golden coat and dark markings shone in the artificial light as her cubs squirmed, fighting each other to latch on to their mother's waiting milk.

The next pen held a black jaguar that eyed her warily, its head down as it sat at the back of its enclosure.

"Are they all like this? Does every cage have a big cat in it?"

"No, just this side." Carstairs pointed out the middle pens, which held what looked like juvenile cats. "When they're big enough they get their own pen while they wait for a booking. Some are kept for breeding, but Buchanan likes to reuse the same ones for that." He looked in disgust in the direction of the old lioness. The poor cat didn't look like she would survive another birth.

RJ studied his face, trying to read his reaction. He didn't meet her eye but she watched as the skin above his collar began to turn a deep red. He was up to his neck in this and he knew it.

He led them around to the other side of the barn. "We've got a variety 'round this side." He sighed deeply and stared at the floor.

RJ and Stuart walked the aisles to find a bear, zebra, wolf, and a huge buffalo that towered over RJ. The buffalo grunted at their presence and RJ instinctively stepped back. It looked like it wanted to charge, its horns terrifying and deadly weapons. The front of the cage was reinforced with steel bars, but that wasn't enough to reassure her. When she turned to see Stuart's pale face, she knew he felt just as vulnerable. The beast swiveled its head to follow them as they backed away, the only movement it could make comfortably in a cage where it wouldn't be able to turn round. Its eyes told a story of the knowledge of its entrapment, a combination of fear mixed with acceptance of its fate. The confronting stare forced RJ's eyes to the ground, and she struggled to swallow the lump that had formed in her throat.

"It's mostly cats," she stated once she found her voice again

"Aye, they're easier to get and to breed." He thumbed towards the side of the building that resembled a lonely ark. "The ones on that side are special orders."

RJ and Stuart looked at each other, neither able to put into words what they were thinking. Carstairs stared at his feet. "Come on," he said. "You need to get that arm seen to."

He led them back to the entranceway where a table and chairs sat waiting in an open area beside a huge sink. The room was barely more than a holding area. Off to the side, RJ could see what looked like a sterile laboratory bathed in darkness: hard white surfaces, stainless steel, and what looked like a microscope on the bench. Hanging inside the door were two tranquilizer-dart rifles.

Stuart followed her gaze. "It looks cleaner in there. Shouldn't we go in there to do it?"

"Aye, right enough. It's restricted access. Only a handful of people are allowed in there. It's the laird's domain. I only have the code in case we need the tranquilizers. I don't really suppose it matters anymore who goes in there. It's over now. It's all over." He closed his eyes, and RJ could practically see the relief wash over him and the tension and stress that he'd been holding leave his body.

He got up and keyed another code into the access pad. The door clicked open. They stepped into the room, then RJ took a seat on a stool while Stuart set about washing his hands with the medical soap at the sink.

When he was done, he examined the wound. "Could've been a lot worse. There's nothing obvious there, but I'll have to clean it out. It'll hurt, but it's necessary." He rifled through the cupboards until he found what he was looking for. After cleaning out a bowl, he filled it with soapy water, then soaked some gauze. As gently as possible, he began to dribble the mixture down RJ's arm and shoulder.

She clenched her jaw at the sting, though it wasn't as bad as she'd expected. But when he gently wiped at the areas surrounding the slashes, getting gradually closer to the wounds, she gripped the table with her good hand and inhaled deeply, gritting her teeth through the pain.

"I've never seen anything like it. It's like ribbon. She cut you up like a grass skirt."

RJ shot him a look that told him to shut up, careful not to look down at her bloody arm.

"What? Not squeamish, are we?"

"Not when it happens to someone else. When it's me that's torn up, it's a different story."

"That'll change," he told her with a hint of sadness in his voice. "You won't always have a partner to sort you out. There's been more than one occasion when I've had to dig a bullet out of my thigh or sew a knife wound up."

"Enough already!" RJ barked as Carstairs's eyes went wide at the thought. "Save your stories from another time. When you're not sewing up someone's arm, for example."

Stuart held his hands up and grimaced, "Sorry, sometimes it helps to talk, that's all."

"Not in this case," RJ assured him. She flicked her eyes towards the shocked gamekeeper.

"Oh right, I was in the army," he reassured Carstairs. "I'm not some sort of mad psycho." He chuckled, which didn't exactly help his case, but Carstairs's eyes gradually returned to normal.

Stuart washed and refilled the bowl too many times for RJ to count. The blood had started to clot, but now it ran down her arm again as he worked, dabbing the area thoroughly with gauze before setting up the suture kit. "I'll do my best, but you're going to have some pretty impressive scars and one hell of a story that, unfortunately, you won't be able to tell anyone."

Carstairs stood by, watching as he ran his cap through his hands in front of him. "I am sorry, Miss."

"I just don't get it, Wullie. All this, and now you're helping us. What's going on? It can't just be a crisis of conscience, not now. That would've come before. If it didn't come when two people died, then why now?"

"None of us are happy about this." He sighed. "You don't understand. Gamekeeping is all I've ever known. I've worked here since I was fourteen and the others have been here since they were teenagers, too. I don't know if you've noticed, but there's not exactly an abundance of jobs around here. We couldn't just up and leave when Buchanan started doing things we didn't agree with. When we raised our concerns, he threatened us, said we were complicit. That we'd go down the same as him, or likely longer as he's the one who can afford the good lawyers. It's not been easy. I'll tell you that much."

He sank to the floor, pulled his knees up, and rested one hand in his hair. The effort of his admission had drained the energy right out of him.

"But you've done nothing to rectify the situation. All you've done is help him run his business. You are complicit."

"No, that's not true. I've had help. We've been trying—"

"The fiscal," RJ exclaimed.

"Aye, the fiscal. Him and I go way back. I knew I could go to him in confidence. He's been looking into the legal side of things while I've been gathering evidence. We want to bring Buchanan down while protecting all the people who work here. It's complicated because he has several police in his pocket."

RJ swallowed past the pain as Stuart concentrated on her sutures. "How did James Sullivan die?" she asked quietly lest she shatter the already broken man in front of her into a million pieces.

"The black panther got him. That's what he asked for, you see. He didn't mind if it was a leopard or a jaguar, just that it was black. He could never have imagined what it would do to him. The dogs found his body the next morning. Half of his skull was torn off." Wullie looked like he was going to be sick. "It was the same one you met this afternoon. We've been trying to find it ever since, but it's evaded us, no matter how hard we've tried to find it. That's never happened before. All the animals have been found before now. They've all been hunted down by their purchasers. This one . . . this one was different."

RJ let him catch his breath and recover. It seemed he needed to get it all out now that he had started.

"Buchanan made us . . . Buchanan made us throw the body headfirst from the ridge. His head smashed like a melon. You wouldn't even have known the thing that lay at the bottom of the cliff was human." He laid his head on his arms, his body heaving as he sobbed.

"The doctor didn't stand a chance, then."

Carstairs shook his head.

Unbelievable, thought RJ. If he'd had any criminal training, the doctor would have suspected something, but the team at the estate had covered their tracks enough to fool the locum, who had no reason to suspect any wrongdoing and certainly no reason to suspect what had actually transpired.

"What about the suicide?" RJ pushed. "Had he had enough of what you were doing or was that a cover up as well?"

"It wasn't a suicide. He was cleaning out the cages when something happened and the door that separates the sides somehow opened. At least, that's what we think happened. It was a mountain lion that ripped out his throat. There was nothing we could do. He was dead when we pulled him out. Buchanan took him out himself and shot him with his own gun. He got rid of any evidence of animal damage by blasting it away with a shotgun."

"He sounds like a cold-hearted bastard."

"I don't know how his father could have produced something like him. When Buchanan Senior died ten years ago, we knew we were in for a rough time, but we never could have imagined . . .

Now, we're wondering if his father didn't die of natural causes."

After learning what Buchanan was capable of, it wouldn't surprise her if he'd committed patricide. "How did it all start? Surely there are other ways of making money off the estate?"

"There is. It's always sustained itself. It's a more common practice than you think, though. There're other estates in poorly populated areas of Britain that do the same. Well, that's what Buchanan told us. But it's not about the money for him. It's about greed and control. Most toffs like him, when they go off to university, they study art history or something else just as airy fairy. He studied zoology. He's been all over the world learning about animals—mainly big cats."

And he still wanted to see them slaughtered. That told her more than anything else Carstairs possibly could.

"He's not right, Miss, something isn't right with his brain. We didn't dare stand up to him. I'm ashamed to say I was afraid of him. If you met him, you'd understand."

RJ nodded, keen to keep Carstairs talking. "What's this room for?" she asked, looking at the impressive array of equipment.

"He inseminates them himself. Likes to play God. It saves him on trips away to replenish stock."

"Is that where he is now, replenishing stock?"

Carstairs nodded. "He's visiting zoos that need to rehome some of their animals. I don't know where—somewhere in Europe. He doesn't explain any of that to us. Just tells us what we need to know . . . and anything that he thinks might make us fear him more."

"Do you know how he manages to obtain them? He must need papers, licenses, and proof of where they're going." RJ was sure zoos wouldn't just give their animals away to anyone offering to take them.

Carstairs looked up at her and shook his head. "I've heard him say that most of these places are desperate and just happy to have the animals taken off their hands. He's fussy, though. He has to see the animals in person, check them out to make sure they're healthy enough to either be hunted or used as baby factories. That's why he goes there himself. That and the power trip, I imagine."

"That's you. Almost good as new." Stuart leaned back to admire his handiwork.

RJ turned her head to look. She doubted it would have been neater or done better if she'd gone to A&E. When their eyes met, RJ sent him a silent message of thanks, which he shrugged off before taking clean gauze and wiping off the remaining blood.

Chapter 26

Carstairs drove them back to their car.

"Thank you, Wullie," RJ said, grasping his hand.

"Well, if it wasn't for you, pet." He shook his head and swallowed down a sob that threatened to escape his throat. "Those wee boys wouldn't have stood a chance. We'd never have made it up to the ridge in time if you hadn't distracted her."

"It's over now."

"Aye," said Carstairs wistfully.

He'd played his part in all of it, even if under duress. None of them could be sure what was about to come his way. Whatever happened, he would always have those deaths and the day's near misses on his conscience.

Stuart shook Wullie's hand, then they got into the car and drove away. In the side mirror, RJ watched the lone figure of Wullie Carstairs get smaller and smaller as he stood staring at their retreating car.

Once out of the estate, Stuart pulled over and phoned in what they had found. The conversation was short and terse when Stuart finished detailing what had happened.

"Yes, yes, I understand . . . okay . . . but—yes." He put the phone down and slammed the flat of his hand against the steering wheel. "We're done."

"What do you mean?"

"That's it. Case closed. They'll send a report to the Chief Constable of Police Scotland, go right to the top, so they can deal with Buchanan, but that's us done. We found out what happened. Everything else now goes through official channels."

"If Buchanan gets word somehow, he'll run. He'll never be held accountable."

"I know, but there's nothing we can do now. It's out of our hands."

"Like hell there isn't." She wasn't going to give up without a fight on this one. They had to get to Buchanan. It wasn't over. They had to finish it.

She winced as she pulled her own phone out of her pocket.

"What're you doing?" he asked.

"There are advantages to having family at the top."

She looked to gauge his reaction. He appeared to be fighting a battle within himself. She knew it was a hard choice for him. He was a soldier; he followed orders, and it went against every bone in his body to go against a superior. But she also knew he wanted to catch Buchanan.

"This'll make life difficult for us, you know that? You, more so. No one's going to want to work with you after this. It's only one step down from going rogue."

"I don't much like having a partner anyway." She informed him with a smile. "And as for the teams at HQ . . ." She shrugged. "Some things are more important than having an easy life. Not that you could call any of what we do easy."

She looked at him and raised her eyebrow in question. She wouldn't do anything without his agreement. It wasn't just her own career that would be affected.

Stuart looked skyward and gulped down some air. He looked straight ahead and nodded. "I'm going to regret this, I know I am."

RJ smiled. If she hadn't been in so much pain, she'd have leaned over and kissed him. Instead, she keyed in the private number for Benjamin Stone, Director of Kingfisher Enterprises.

#

Benjamin looked at the caller ID on his phone. RJ was calling him. She was the only employee in the organization who had a direct line to his office.

Everyone else had to go through Martha before getting to him—if they even got that far. He was far too busy to talk to every agent, and Martha was generally able to sort out any issues that came to his office over the phone.

"Hey," he said, picking up the phone in an instant, worried as he always was when RJ phoned him on assignment.

"Hey," came the reply. He could hear the relief in her voice with just that one word.

He got straight to the point. "I take it this isn't a social call, since you're phoning the office phone."

"It's not," RJ confirmed. "But I sure am glad to hear your voice."

"As am I. What can I do for you?"

RJ outlined their findings, what they had been told to do, and finally what she actually wanted to do as Benjamin listened to her speech in its entirety.

"Where is Buchanan now?" he asked when she had finished.

"We don't know. We'll need some resources to help us ascertain that."

Benjamin closed his eyes as he considered her request. He started his Newton's Cradle as he ran through options in his head. If he allowed her this request, her career could be irreparably damaged.

"Okay," he told her after what seemed like an eternity but was actually only a few seconds. "I'll put a new team on it. The other team will never know about them. I'll pave the way here. You just get Buchanan and take him down. Await new orders."

"Thanks, Ben."

"Take care, RJ."

"Yeah, about that . . ."

"What?" asked her uncle, suddenly concerned.

"Nothing, its fine."

There was the slightest hitch in her voice that told him it was not, in fact, nothing.

"I'll explain everything when I see you."

He sighed. "Are you sure you're okay?"

"Yes, and I'll be a hell of a lot better once we have Buchanan."

"Okay."

Benjamin's mind was already onto the next thing before he even hit the disconnect button on the phone. He immediately connected to Martha's desk. "Get me the handler in charge of RJ's assignment." Martha held all of the current, and much of the past, working information of everything about the organization in her head. He was connected in seconds.

He dispensed with any pleasantries and launched straight into the reason for his call. "Hold fire on the police report on James Sullivan's death. We've got some agents currently on the ground in the country where Buchanan is. We're going to bring him in ourselves as a special favor to Governor Kowalski."

"Yes sir," came the reply. "Will there be anything else?"

"No, and thank you for your work." He hung up and buzzed Martha to come in, detailing to her what he wanted when she appeared.

She smirked as he explained what was going on.

"What, you don't approve?" he asked. In the grand scheme of things, it didn't matter if she did or not—he was the director after all. He valued her input, though, even if it wasn't always what he wanted to hear.

"That's not the case at all," she told him. "Seems your niece will do anything to ensure she gets the desired results, using all means available to her. If that's not the sign of a good agent, I don't know what is."

"Yes," he agreed and shook his head, "I suppose it is."

"I'll get it organized right away." She hurried from his office and left him to ponder what she had just said.

#

Five hours later, RJ and Stuart were on a plane at Glasgow Airport waiting to take off. RJ had left her shoulder exposed during their drive down but had covered it with a light silk scarf Stuart had picked up at a tourist shop on the drive down. Stuart's face was not as easy to disguise but it had been a number of days since his accident and the wound had started to heal. Huge parts of the scab had flaked off to leave shiny pink skin underneath. The rest was dark and dry, and attracted attention wherever he went. His limp, although less pronounced than it had been before, added to the effect. He'd had to explain to everyone about his 'mountaineering accident', from the check-in clerk to security to the little curious boy who sat beside his mother across the aisle from them. After asking Stuart about it, the little boy continued to stare until his mother diverted his attention outside to the baggage train.

"You know that story isn't going to work when we get over there."

Stuart remained silent.

"It's bad enough that we'll have to go through it all again at the next airport for our connecting flight and then when we arrive—"

"I know." Stuart looked dejected. "If we need to go in quiet, then you go alone. I'll just have to provide you with remote back-up. It might prove to be useful. It's a good thing."

"Why do you look more deflated than the kid who always gets picked last for sports than someone who actually believes that?"

RJ squeezed his arm and stared at him, forcing him to meet her eye. He couldn't help but smile. The change in the shape of his face amplified the crusty scabs that were left, parts of which looked like they could fall at any moment. The effect was just shy of terrifying.

She must have looked disgusted, or at the very least unnerved, because he asked, "Not that bad, am I?"

"Probably worse than when you first asked me that question when you woke up the day after the fall. Maybe if you just . . ." RJ mimed pulling at her face.

"Nope, no chance. It'll scar if I start pulling bits off. Besides, looking like this could be much more fun."

RJ looked out of the window. She was experiencing a vague sense of relief to be leaving

Scotland, which was unexpected. She'd been okay to fly into the country, but now that she was leaving, a weight lifted from her shoulders. Perhaps it was the idea that they were going to get Buchanan—or partly that, at least.

Her phone pinged with an update from HQ.

"They've tracked his phone to a hotel," she told Stuart. So far all they'd had to go on was a record of his travel arrangements. Now, they had narrowed it down. "They're attempting to find out if there are any nearby zoos or animal parks looking to relocate any animals."

Stuart chewed on his lip. It had already started to bleed and added to his crazed look. "And a recent photo?"

RJ handed him her phone, which showed an overweight man in his early forties with a receding hairline and well-manicured beard that was trimmed close to his face.

"You'd never know if you walked past him on the street."

"No, you wouldn't," she agreed, "Everyone will know soon enough, though."

"Try and get some sleep," Stuart told her. "We'll need it."

They closed their eyes and attempted to power nap. Sleep came more easily to Stuart as RJ struggled to get her thoughts under control and curb the intensity of her pain. She performed some of the breathing exercises she'd been taught at Kingfisher, and soon she was dozing gently. Neither of them was aware when the plane took off for mainland Europe.

By the time they arrived at their destination, they were both recharged and feeling better physically, except for the pain in RJ's arm and shoulder.

"We'll get you something stronger here," Stuart promised her, after seeing her pale and clammy face.

"I'll need it if I'm to go in alone."

"We make a bit of a pair, don't we? No offence. I like you, and I think we've worked well together, but let's not partner up again. I've had enough injuries to last for quite a while around you."

She laughed. "Agreed. But we'll always have Scotland."

"We'll always have Scotland."

"You stay here. I'll get the rental car," RJ told him when they exited the airport.

Stuart nodded and took his phone out. "I'll organize supplies and better pain relief. What we need should already be at the hotel, but I want to make sure we've got the right meds."

RJ didn't argue. She had stumbled as they made their way through immigration, just slightly, but she knew Stuart had seen it.

"And RJ—"

She looked up to meet his eyes.

"I'll be driving when you bring the car around. You need the rest. Buchanan isn't a man to be messed with."

Chapter 27

When they arrived at the zoo, it wasn't at all what RJ had been expecting. She hadn't consciously thought about it, but she had expected some kind of run-down, depressing, unkempt facility, not the bright, clean, vibrant business they pulled into. Raised beds of flowers in every color of the rainbow bowed in a pleasant breeze as they got out of the car. There was barely a space left in the giant car park, but an efficient parking attendant showed them the way to a place for their car. They squeezed out of the vehicle, unable to open the doors properly due to so many cars being crammed into the space.

"I think perhaps you'd better stay here," she told Stuart diplomatically as he opened his door and twisted his way out of the vehicle.

"Right you are. Sorry, I completely forgot." He touched his rough face and a dry crusty flake fell to the ground. Squeezing back into the car, he opened the windows to provide some cross breeze and took out his phone. "Call me if you need me," he told her over his shoulder, but she was already gone.

RJ walked down the pathway that sat in the middle of the car park, amongst chattering children and tired parents. A sudden roar came from the depths of the zoo, making some of the children gasp, while others shrieked in fright or laughed in delight, their expressions mirrored on their parent's faces. Many of the children and adults wore lanyards around their necks. If RJ had been able to read the language, she was certain it would read 'annual pass' or something similar. Business appeared to be booming.

There were queues at four ticket windows and an office to the right. This was where she had been instructed to go. She gave her name to the receptionist and sat down. It seemed zoo computer networks weren't as secure as they could be, or this one's wasn't. Not that it would have made much difference. She was quite sure the hackers-slash-computer systems experts at Kingfisher would have been able to get in anywhere. As it was, it had been relatively simple for them to sneak in the back door and insert an appointment for her with the director of the zoo, just after Buchanan's. It was no error that she'd arrived before him.

The receptionist frowned at her screen, then looked up at RJ before frowning down at her screen again. "Miss—"

"Oh, yes, I know I'm early." RJ waved her hand dismissively.

The woman looked at her in puzzlement. After a second of rummaging about in her desk, she beckoned RJ over and tried to give her a pass, pointing out the door and tapping her watch.

RJ smiled and shook her head, holding up her hands. She pointed back to her seat and took out her phone. The receptionist shrugged and smiled, sitting back down.

RJ scrolled through her phone and tried to look busy.

The receptionist clicked away on her keyboard until a bulky shadow crossed the doorway. Buchanan strolled in and greeted her with a smile and his name. The receptionist smiled back and directed him to a seat. As he sat down across from her, RJ looked up. They politely acknowledged each other.

In his three-piece suit, he looked like any other respectable businessman—or even an academic. RJ, on the other hand, was dressed in gray trousers and a short-sleeved beige shirt with Winchester Animal Park embroidered on the pocket. The efficiency of the organization in making arrangements and sourcing clothing never ceased to amaze her. She'd found it waiting for her in the room when they went to check in.

"Winchester. English, eh?" Buchanan asked, nodding towards her shirt, his double chin leaning on his collar.

"Why, yes," she replied in a faux English accent that she felt sure he would see right through. "And you?"

"Scotland. Got a park in need of some big cats. Perfect weather for them just now," he joked. "They'd be right at home."

"Forgive me for saying, but your accent is very light."

"Went to boarding school, then uni down in England, traveled the world some before going back to the family home. I can't quite place yours, either."

"No? We moved around a lot when I was younger," RJ replied but Buchanan had already lost interest. He balanced an argyle-covered ankle on his opposite knee and relaxed back in his chair before checking his watch. His appointment was running late.

A door opened further down the corridor and two men came striding up. "Thank you for that, Günter," said the elder, shaking the younger man's hand. "It certainly is something to consider." The young man had no clue as to what RJ saw as obvious—whatever he had asked for was never going to be granted, not in a million years. The men said their goodbyes and the elder turned to the receptionist, who spoke quietly to him in their own language.

When he turned back around to face them, he had a huge fake smile plastered on his face "Ah, Mr. Buchanan, how very nice to meet you. Won't you come on through?"

Buchanan stood to shake his hand, and as he did, RJ also stood. Buchanan stopped mid-shake and looked at her in confusion.

"Mr. Petrov, Riley Black from Winchester Animal Park. I see you're running late and wonder if I might make a suggestion."

Petrov looked at her in curiosity. Buchanan's expression was quickly turning to one of suppressed anger.

"It seems both myself and Mr. Buchanan are here with the same business in mind. Perhaps we should combine the meetings? Save us all some time. After all, we're all here for the same purpose. For the benefit of the animals."

Petrov directed a bright and toothy smile towards her. "A splendid idea. That is, if you have no objections, Mr. Buchanan?" He raised his eyebrows in question.

Buchanan had little choice but to agree. His tight-lipped smile and the daggers in his eyes, however, told a different story.

Once they were in the director's office, he pulled a plastic chair over to join the leather chair in front of his desk. RJ chose the leather and pulled it closer to the desk, putting Buchanan at a disadvantage before he even sat down.

"I understand you have some cats that require new homes," RJ started as soon as their bottoms hit the chairs, keen to gain the upper hand in the conversation, as well as the position in the room.

"Yes, yes, we do." Petrov looked down at the papers in front of him. "Miss Black, would you tell me a bit about your establishment? I'm afraid I'm not familiar with it."

"Certainly." RJ smiled her most charming smile. "We're a rather new park. Just three years old." She rattled off the facts supplied to her from the newly set-up webpage that someone at Kingfisher had managed to rattle up in the last twenty-four hours. "My husband and I set it up together. The aim of our park is education. It's all about inspiring young people about nature and the best ways we can look after the valuable resource that is our planet. As such, I'm sure you can understand that we need some way to pull people in, attract attention to our park. We've invested heavily in our big cat section.

It was important for us to get it right before we started sourcing animals. We've just recently finished, hence why I'm here."

She looked at Buchanan.

"And Mr. Buchanan, you've already explained about your safari park when we spoke on the phone," Petrov offered.

"Safari park? Are you planning on letting them roam, Mr. Buchanan?" she asked him, watching to gauge his reaction to the idea.

Without missing a beat, Buchanan answered, "Not roam, my dear. A select few of our animals are held in larger enclosures. We also have an area where people can visit our animals in carefully built habitats." He directed his attention to Petrov again. "I have the plans here, if you'd like to look." He shook the document holder in Petrov's direction. Petrov smiled indulgently, and Buchanan, keen to impress, unscrewed the lid with a flourish. He rolled out the plans on the desk in front of them.

RJ could see Petrov was immediately impressed. He took in the ponds and the waterfalls, the native trees, hidey holes in a faux rock face, and natural stimulations of every kind imaginable. "The space that you must have to do something of this size and scope, Mr. Buchanan.

I must say, these are inspiring. Who did you have design these for you?"

"I did them myself, Mr. Petrov. I've been refining these ideas for years. These animals only deserve the best. I aim to give it to them."

RJ wondered if she'd have been able to see through Buchanan's act if she didn't already know what a power-hungry, ruthless liar he was. The plans were a nice touch. No doubt he had different plans drawn up for each type of cat and other animals—designs that were so well-suited to each animal that they couldn't fail to impress a zoo looking to rehome its animals.

Petrov looked up from the plans and smiled at each of them. "As you know, our leopard Kano gave birth eighteen months ago to five healthy cubs—very unusual and very lucky for us. A great example of the work we do at this zoo." His chest puffed out with pride. "We are due to exchange one for another in Australia to give us diversity in our breeding program; another is already earmarked for another zoo, which means we have three left." He made a few clicks on his computer and turned the screen to show them a live video feed of the cubs currently in their sleeping pen, climbing all over each other, biting, clawing and doing just about everything but sleep.

"They look remarkably healthy. Beautiful animals. I can take two off your hands," Buchanan stated. "As you can see from my plans, I have two enclosures side by side. Once the cubs are ready to be separated, I can give them the space that they need."

"It's highly unusual that we send two to the same facility," Petrov said, frowning slightly.

"Do any other facilities have habitats as impressive as this one?" Buchanan asked.

RJ figured Buchanan possessed the same knowledge Kingfisher had passed onto her. Petrov had been trying, unsuccessfully, since the cubs were born, to find suitable new homes for them all. They were nearing the age where they needed to be separated from their mother and Petrov had neither the space nor the resources to keep them at their current home.

Petrov rubbed his chin and looked at Buchanan's designs again.

"Mr. Petrov?" RJ tentatively stuck her finger in the air to get his attention.

He looked up and blinked, as if he'd forgotten she was in the room.

"My park specializes in big cats. I can assure you of no better home for Kano's offspring. We'll take all three and provide a generous donation to your zoo."

Buchanan stared at her, his face flushed red. "Now, hang on there a minute."

"How generous?" asked Petrov.

Running a zoo was an expensive business, even one as popular as this one. RJ wagered on the assumption that animal welfare was a top priority for Petrov, but money was a close second. She set her jaw, and watching Buchanan in her periphery vision, focused her gaze on Petrov. "One hundred thousand pounds."

She saw him do a quick calculation in his head as Buchanan tried to pick his jaw up from the floor.

"You have a deal, Miss Black," Petrov told her with a self-satisfied smile.

"Fantastic, I'll be in touch to make the arrangements." She stood, shook his hand, nodded curtly to Buchanan and walked out the door.

She didn't get far across the car park before Buchanan caught up with her. His meaty hand grabbed her shoulder and forced her to turn to face him.

"Just what do you think you're playing at?" he blustered, almost spitting on her in his anger. "We could both have gotten animals there. You didn't have to go and pull the rug from under me like that. Winchester Animal Park? There's no such place. I know every animal park in the UK. What's your game here?"

"No, there isn't a Winchester Animal Park, but I'd do anything to make sure you didn't get your grubby little paws on those leopard cubs or any other animals."

Buchanan's face was scarlet with rage. RJ flicked a glance over his shoulder as Stuart approached. Luckily, Buchanan was too worked up to notice, and within in a second, Stuart plunged a syringe in Buchanan's neck.

Chapter 28

A large crate arrived in front of the home of the Metropolitan Police—ironically called, in this case, New Scotland Yard—in the early hours of the morning two days after RJ's trip to the zoo. A forklift delivered the crate, then disappeared inside the bowels of a nondescript white truck that casually made its way through the streets of London. No record of the truck was ever found. Somehow, any CCTV in the vicinity malfunctioned and started to replay an image showing one hour previously. Only those watching extremely carefully would have noticed, but with banks of screens to watch, no one noticed anything on the cold and foggy morning after the heatwave had finally blown over. It would have been preferable to drop the crate off at the Headquarters of Police Scotland at Tulliallan, but it was far easier to disappear in London. The MET would soon transfer the contents. An added bonus was the publicity the London drop-off would generate.

The unusual object soon caught the attention of passersby and of the occupants in New Scotland Yard, who cautiously came out to investigate. The air holes caused much conjecture as to its contents, but, all in all, everyone who saw it was completely puzzled as to what it was and how it had managed to arrive undetected.

They cordoned the area off to keep the public at bay before visually examining the exterior of the crate, careful not to get too close. What they found was a large black stamp on all sides detailing the contents to be a dangerous animal. No documentation was attached and no sounds came from the crate.

The bomb squad was called to investigate further, and the cordons were pushed back as a remote robot slowly approached the wooden box and gently inserted a small camera into one of the holes on the north side.

A crowd of police personnel gathered around the handheld computer that the operator held. The camera swiveled round to give a better view of the interior. "Is that . . . is that human?"

"Looks to be," replied another of the bomb officers as he squinted at the image. He took off his glasses to check that his mind wasn't playing tricks on him, then put them back on.

"Dead?"

"Unable to tell."

The camera was taken out and reinserted in various holes to ensure that there were no hidden bombs or booby traps. Once it was decided that the crate was safe, an officer was sent off to find a crowbar. The same officer had the luck to lever open the lid, knowing what he would find but at the same time completely oblivious to whom the box contained.

A doctor stood by and leaned in as soon as the top was off. He checked the occupant's pulse, which was beating strongly, and motioned to the crime-scene photographers to step in quickly before an ambulance took the man away, although not before a member of the forensics team removed the manila envelope that had been pinned to the front of the unconscious man's shirt.

The contents of the envelope detailed who the man was, his crimes, and the contact details of a Fiscal Alexander Dunn who should be called upon to provide evidence of the man's illegal activities. A letter at the back of the substantial information pack gave the name of a previously unknown animal rights organization—Animal Solidarity Society or ASS for short—as the senders of the data and the rest of the contents of the crate.

A document in the pack stated that the crate was identical to the ones Buchanan used to ship his animals, from the straw on the floor and the air holes on all sides, to the water that was supplied, and the drug used to induce sleep and make for easy transportation. This information was phoned through to the hospital as soon as it was found, but by that time, the man had woken up groggy and was demanding to speak to his lawyer.

The police stationed outside his door relayed the information back to their superiors, who agreed that the man should speak to his lawyer and that he would need a damn good one to get out of the fix he was in. They all agreed that even the best lawyer in the country wouldn't be able to get him out of it. The man was sure to go to prison for a long time.

No information could be found on the elusive Animal Solidarity Society. A single recent graduate from the Police College was assigned to the task. He found little, other than a very generic website that contained only one page—a page that summarized the crimes Buchanan had committed. The website could not be traced, which seemed unusual for such a simply designed site. The new recruit didn't give it much thought, and soon he was reassigned to help crack a terrorist plot to blow up the offices of BBC Scotland. One lone officer had investigated the society for less than five hours. Far more resources had been used to investigate the crimes laid out in the package the society had provided.

#

At the exact same time that the crate was delivered, a small bundle of black crawled out from a cave on an estate in Scotland and opened its sleep-shut eyes against the rising sun of the morning. It looked back and mewled. Another bundle, identical to the first, wobbled out on shaky legs. A rabbit took fright at the sudden noise, shooting out from behind a fragrant gorse bush, and the cubs gave chase. The rabbit was far too quick and darted this way and that before finding a hole and plunging down into the safe dark of the burrow below.

The little black cats came up short at the hole, far too big to follow the rabbit down. The first swatted his paw ineffectually inside the hole; his brother caught sight of another rabbit and went after it. The first soon followed. It was days later before they made their first kill. They tore at it and ate the meat, ravenously, fighting over the last few pieces. A day later, they caught another and the next day another still. As they got better at the hunt, they got bigger in size.

#

RJ was glad she had been on a plane flying home across the Atlantic when the crate was discovered and consequently reported in the press. She hoped it would give her uncle and the others at Kingfisher time to calm down and view the situation logically. No such luck. There were twelve messages waiting for her when the plane touched down and she turned her phone on. She didn't bother listening to the messages, but a text came through, ordering her to go straight to HQ and Benjamin's office when she arrived.

For once, she was through the airport in a flash. Unfortunately, there was no line for taxis at the stand and traffic seemed inexplicably quiet. She was deposited on the footpath in front of the building in record time, on the one day when she was in no hurry to get there. She rubbed the back of her neck. The muscles there had tightened up on the plane ride and now felt like knot upon knot. She trudged up the stairs and swiped her security pass. Those inside would know she had arrived. Thankfully, there was no one in the elevator. She knew that no one except her handlers and a small team were aware which case she'd been on or her connection to the huge news story of the day, but she still shrunk slightly at the thought of bumping into anyone as she made her way towards a reprimanding, like a guilty child heading to the headmaster's office.

She steeled herself before she walked in to the outer office. Martha's polite greeting gave nothing away. She waved her straight through. RJ lifted her chin, threw back her shoulders, and attempted to stride confidently in to her awaiting uncle.

He glowered at her from behind his desk and his steepled fingers, which were never a good sign.

She sat in the chair across from him. It seemed lower than she remembered, but perhaps it was just her imagination. She wouldn't have put it past him to lower the setting for occasions such as this, though, just to emphasize the real balance of power. Waiting to hear him speak was painful.

"The showboating, was it really necessary?" he asked her at last.

"I thought so."

"The governor has already been on the phone. He was not at all pleased with how things have turned out, especially as he made it clear we were to be discreet." He gave her a pointed look.

"The whole hunting thing would have come out anyway whenever or however Buchanan went to trial. Which will take at least six months. It's better it came out now instead of during any sensitive election processes. The governor's office has the chance to get ahead of it and deal with the issue before all that happens. Buchanan deserved what he got. The worse thing he would want to deal with is that public loss of face. He feeds off power, so we cut him off at the source. It'll be a stark warning to whoever else decides to branch off in the same line of business. Plus, we had to make it all about him. Those around him should be protected. He needed to be seen as the one that organized it all, which he was." She stopped, breathless, lest she start rambling. Somehow it had all sounded better in her head when she had rehearsed it on the plane. She looked up at her uncle through her long lashes and waited for his response.

He sighed. "That's very similar to what I said to Governor Kowalski."

"So, he's okay with it all?"

"No, he's not okay with it all, and I doubt he'll be using our services in the near future, but he is grateful that you found his brother-in-law's killer. Janice Sullivan is threatening to go over and tear through Buchanan in much the same manner as the panther that killed her husband. No, the governor isn't okay with it, but he has more than enough on his plate to contend with at the moment."

A rabid Janice Sullivan was more than enough for anyone to deal with—RJ knew that better than most.

"And are we okay?" she asked him tentatively.

"Yes, of course we're okay." He stood up and moved around his desk to give her a hug. "We'll always be okay. Always."

They squeezed each other tight, and a tear escaped from the corner of RJ's eye.

"Just promise me that next time, before you go making any grand-standing public displays, you'll at least call in to speak to me.

"I will. I promise."

He released her, but they remained standing, both wanting to be close to the other.

"Don't get too comfy," he told her. "You've got forty-eight hours leave before you're off on another assignment."

"That soon?" Her shoulders slumped in disappointment. She had been hoping for some downtime to let her shoulder heal. She still hadn't told Benjamin about it, but it seemed to be healing nicely. Some R&R would also have been good in terms of spending time with her dear old uncle. It would have been good to remind him that she was much more than just a whole lot of trouble and bother.

"Probably best to keep the troublesome boss's niece out of sight and out of mind for a while. Governor Kowalski was more understanding than some other employees in the know, or so Martha informs me."

"Yes, right. Well. I guess another assignment isn't a bad idea, then."

He nodded dramatically. "You're going to be the death of me, girl, you really are."

"So, where am I off to now? Tell me more."

"Well . . ."

Chapter 29

The court case was held in Glasgow at the High Court of Justiciary six months later. Because of the volume of public interest in the case around the world, the press descended on the building and the surrounding streets but were not permitted to enter the courtroom. The public benches were packed on the first few weeks of trial, which RJ had anticipated. She hadn't wanted to hear all the details again—she knew full well what had happened and experienced firsthand far more than most in the court room. She did attend on the last day, flying in the night before and arriving early to ensure a seat, hidden surreptitiously at the back. Stuart wasn't there. She hadn't expected him to be. If it wasn't for a serendipitous break between assignments—serendipity she was sure her uncle had something to do with—she might not have attended herself.

Janice Sullivan sat sobbing quietly, dressed in black as she had been on each day of the trial, evidenced by a multitude of news channels as their cameras caught her leaving from the court each day.

On this day, she was not alone. Her brother, the imposing figure of Governor Mike Kowalski, clutched her hand. He had braved the media storm surprisingly well after James Sullivan's real cause of death had been exposed. Feigning complete ignorance of his brother-in-law's big game hunting had helped a little, as had his public condemnation of the practice, but what had been the bigger contributing factor was his large donation to a series of ventures that set to protect wildlife in Africa and South America. Polls put him as a dead cert to be re-elected the following year.

The siblings stared at the back of Buchanan's head throughout the morning's proceedings. His stiff neck did not move an inch, but it colored a deeper red as the hours went on. Whether this was embarrassment or anger, it was impossible to say.

It was noon when the jury was led off to make their deliberations. As RJ made to leave, a hand caught her cuff from behind. She turned to find Wullie Carstairs, looking ten years younger and a hell of a lot happier.

"You should stick around, Miss. They're not expecting it to take long."

RJ smiled with affection at the man who had saved her life. "Thank you, Wullie, I think I will."

She turned to move off again, but caught herself and turned back. "Do you have time for a cup of tea?"

He smiled and his face was instantly transformed. "I'd like that very much, Miss Black."

"That's not really—"

"I figured that," he interrupted her, "but let's just stick to what we know, eh?"

RJ nodded and led him to a café a few minutes' walk away. It was a café she had seen many times before on her way to the university, but she'd never been inside. They found a seat easily enough, although the line for takeaway coffee was long and filled with media crews keen to get their fix.

They were silent until they were seated, unsure of how to broach their complicated shared history.

"How are things up at the estate?" she asked him.

"Good, good. It's a different place up there now. No more sheep attacks, for one. The only bodies we find now are rabbits. Bloody foxes. Not that we want the rabbits, either. It's all ticking over."

"And you and the others? You aren't being charged."

"No." He shook his head and sighed in relief. "The fiscal was able to argue our position to the Crown and they decided not to prosecute. They saw who the real one to blame was and probably decided it was better to spend the money on bringing him to justice than to involve his lackeys who had no real choice but to follow orders." He wound his hands together. Whatever relief Buchanan's apprehension had given him, RJ could only imagine how stressful the last few weeks and today had to be.

"I'm glad you got through this in one piece," RJ told him. "It could have been very different. For a whole lot of us," she added.

"I still have nightmares about that now. Those wee boys . . ."

RJ watched him struggle with the internal torture.

"Speaking of which, how have the rest of the community been with you? Not exactly a good look to almost get the publican's children killed."

"No, it's not," he agreed. "Tracy was fine with it, though. She's a good woman. I explained it to her the night I went down after the boys. She was pretty shocked but agreed to keep it quiet. It helped that she knew it was all about to come out, plus she didn't want the boys to go through the horror of reliving it."

"You told her?" said RJ and she almost choked on her tea.

"It wasn't right not to. Those boys could have been traumatized and they needed to be able to talk about what happened. They're seeing a counselor now and seem to be on the mend." He looked wistful and suddenly reddened.

"There's something you're not telling me," RJ pushed gently.

He swallowed and looked ready to start speaking but hesitated and stopped himself.

RJ waited.

"We're to be married come spring." He cast his eyes down, abashed.

"Who?" RJ asked, not sure she was quite understanding.

"Myself and Tracy."

RJ tried and only just succeeded in stopping her jaw hitting the floor. If there was ever a more unlikely couple, she'd never come across them. The age difference alone must have been twenty years. Not that she was judging, but it was a bit of a surprise.

"Wow, congratulations." She got out of her seat to give him a hug. "How on earth did that happen?"

"I suppose I was spending a bit more time there, checking on the boys, and well . . . Her man's been out of the picture for a while," he explained, keen not to darken his good character—or more likely Tracy's.

"Well, I'm very happy for you both. For all of you. Here's to new beginnings." She held up her tea cup and clinked it against his.

Wullie, satisfied that he wasn't about to be labeled a cradle snatcher, got stuck into the cream pancake that had just been deposited in front of him on the table.

RJ had chosen the same. She wondered about the last time she'd had one—probably not since she was little, and this one was just as good as she remembered. Proper comfort food. It was just what they both needed, in their own very different ways. They enjoyed the experience in companionable silence, until RJ swallowed her last bite. "What'll happen up at the estate if Buchanan is sent to jail?"

"When he's sent to jail. Funny thing that. It was all easier than we could have ever expected. Soon after his very public arrest . . ." He stared at her, looking for confirmation that she had something to do with it, but she remained silent and still, a tiny smile curling up the corners of her mouth. ". . . the family solicitor turned up at our door, asking questions."

"So he could help Buchanan?"

"No, this one represents the interests of the estate. The Buchanans have been using the firm for years, which itself has been handed down through the family. Oldest firm in Oban. Anyway, turns out there's a stipulation in the old man's will. There has been in every will since there've been Buchanans on that land." He took a sip of his tea to draw out the tension. "Turns out, if one of them is convicted of any crimes, he loses his hereditary rights and the estate is passed on to the next in line."

RJ was puzzled. "But what does that mean? I thought he was an only child." Kingfisher had looked closely into Buchanan's background so she knew he had no family that could inherit in his place.

"Oh, he was."

RJ's eyebrows knitted together as she frowned in his direction. She could see Wullie was enjoying this.

He put her out of her misery. "Turns out Buchanan had an illegitimate child seven years ago. His name wasn't on the birth certificate, but he'd had a DNA test to prove she was his. No one knew about her except the solicitor. Buchanan never had anything to do with her except to send a measly support payment to her mother once a month. They were down in Govan, living in a wee council house, while Buchanan was living it up on the estate and flying all over the world."

"But a seven-year-old can't be put in charge of the estate, surely?"

"Aye, you're right there. That's the best bit. It'll be held in trust for her and run on her behalf until she reaches twenty-one."

RJ grinned. "And you're going to run the place?"

"Aye. The paperwork's all waiting to be signed as soon as Buchanan's sentenced. Then the girl and her mother will move up to the big house and into her rightful life. It'll piss Buchanan off to no end. Be the final nail in the coffin, so to speak." His eyes glittered in glee. For an instant, she saw the little rascal she'd seen in the school photo standing beside the boy who would become Fiscal Alexander Dunn.

His phone started to ring and interrupted his revelry.

The call was short and sweet. "Hello. Aye. Right. Bye." He put the phone back in his pocket and looked back up at RJ, who was waiting with bated breath. "They're calling us back in. We'd better go."

"That was quick."

"Aye, it was. Let's hope the jury makes the right decision."

Epilogue

They did. All fifteen jurors gave the verdict as guilty. The judge listened to the plea in mitigation given by Buchanan's solicitor as he desperately tried to aid his client in the sentencing. He fought a losing battle. The judge sentenced Buchanan to thirty years, with six months served already. He based his decisions on the two culpable homicides, perverting the course of justice in covering up the deaths, a number of crimes under the Dangerous Wild Animal Act, and public endangerment. Although he was supposed to be completely objective, the fact that Buchanan was so obviously a vile human being likely bore some weight in the judge's heavy sentencing—heavy for Scotland, at least.

Thirty years. Buchanan would get out, but not for a long time, and when he did, he would have nothing. No family, no inheritance, no life.

Buchanan was led out of the court and into the back of a waiting transport van, his face as white as a sheet, the only person surprised at the verdict.

Janice Sullivan kept it together for the verdict and the subsequent sentencing. She held her head up high and walked out of the court to the waiting reporters, keen to be the one who broke the news. She didn't appear to see the irony that her husband had been complicit in the crime that led to his death. For her, Buchanan was an evil villain who had stolen away the love of her life.

Seven-year-old Daisy Buchanan, moved into her new home three months later. The staff loved her, and she them. The bright little girl and her mother breathed new life into the big house and the rest of the estate. She'd turn out to be the best thing that ever happened there.

The rabbit population on the estate was finally under control, through no efforts of the employees there. Something seemed to be killing them off, but no foxes were seen or heard, and so a virus of sorts was given credit for the population control. The saying 'don't look a gift horse in the mouth' came quickly to the lips of anyone on the estate whenever someone mentioned it. They'd all had enough to deal with for the last few years without looking for problems.

Meanwhile, the two little cubs were growing strong and powerful. They remained wary of humans and human sounds. Their mother had taught them well before she'd disappeared from their lives. At night, they sat in the moonlight on the rock outside their cave and surveyed the land that stretched out before them, their stomachs full. They'd soon have to start venturing further to hunt—their rabbit supply was dwindling and they needed more. The bigger beast twitched his ear as a moth landed on his head and began to explore his soft fur. These they could handle, but midges . . . midges were the only downside to an otherwise perfect life.

The Festival Killer

Agent RJ Rox is in charge of her first case for the clandestine organization known as Kingfisher. A ticking clock and a colleague who could make the whole assignment blow up in her face, pile on the pressure in a case that seems impossible to crack. An ambassador's secret love child, gone missing at the Berlin Book Festival years previously, lead her in a direction she never could have imagined . . . and back to the streets of Scotland.

As RJ searches for answers, she learns the truth is stranger than fiction when she sets her sights on a world-famous crime writer. Does a new book hold the key to the whole case, and can RJ unlock it in time?

RJ's playing a deadly game with a killer who has something to prove—almost as much as she has.

About the author

Jo McCready grew up on the rain-soaked streets of small town Scotland before moving to the sunnier climes of Auckland, New Zealand in 2010. She has a background in psychology, and a lifetime love of mystery and murder.

Sign up for all her latest news at jomccready.com

Printed in Great Britain
by Amazon